Jackson pushed open the door and was met with a breathtaking sight—long feminine legs leading upward to a curvaceous bottom encased in snug shorts. Concentrating on her unpacking, she didn't notice his entrance. Each move she made tightened the fabric across her hips. His pulse quickened. This could prove interesting.

"Hello, *cher*. I'm Jackson. Welcome to the team."

Her back stiffened, and she dropped what she had in her arms. She stood upright and slowly turned around.

Jackson had only a moment to catch his breath before he came face-to-face with his past. Here was the reason for his unease. Her glossy brown hair hung to her chin where it curled under and hugged her cheeks. That stubborn chin lifted into the air with challenge. Her eyes sparked blue fire, and shadowed pain haunted their depths as she gave him a straightforward look. At five feet, nine inches, she was tall but still had to look up at him. His heart nearly stopped and then began to race frantically.

"Charlie! You're dead," he blurted.

A Flame Rekindled

by

Evelyn Timidaiski

Brandon's Brigade, Book 2

A Flame Rekindled

Contact Information: info@thewildrosepress.com

Cover Art by *Kristian Norris*

The Wild Rose Press, Inc.
PO Box 708
Adams Basin, NY 14410-0708
Visit us at www.thewildrosepress.com

Publishing History
First Edition, 2023
Trade Paperback ISBN 978-1-5092-5291-6
Digital ISBN 978-1-5092-5292-3

Brandon's Brigade, Book 2
Published in the United States of America

Dedication

To James, with love.

Chapter One

Clear skies and emerald seas painted the cockpit window as Jackson Favre banked the plane and began his descent. As he did, his New Orleans *Mojo* kicked in. He rubbed the back of his hand where an itch nagged at him.

Raised in the swamps of Louisiana outside *The Big Easy*, he firmly believed in the premonitions that had plagued him since childhood. Mostly a nuisance or embarrassment as a youth, the special sight had proved invaluable when he had served as a Navy SEAL. Now, he wondered what surprise awaited him below.

He was returning from the bayous of home which had included a stop off in Shreveport, Louisiana to get a much-needed paint job for his plane, *Darlin*.

The last mission had resulted in a score of bullet holes marring the plane's shiny canary paint. Besides, Brandon, his former SEAL team leader, had insisted the bright yellow made the craft look like a sitting duck in the water. The new military green was more appropriate for their covert operations, if less appealing. Though he had quarters at the homestead, the refurbished World War II Grumman served as Jackson's home as well as the Brigade's transport plane.

Coffee Island, dubbed *Café Caye* by the locals, came into view. A jolt of affection for the old coffee plantation surprised him. The place already felt like home. He dipped the plane's wing in respect for the beauty before him.

Covered in pristine jungle, the twenty-mile by thirty-mile island served as a training ground for *Brandon's Brigade.* The new project was a major undertaking, and Jackson was lucky to take his little break before the real work started. The Brigade was a fledgling, still requiring lots of TLC and elbow grease.

The sea darkened to a richer blue as he flew over the deeper waters on the east side of the island. Lush, forested mountains rose like guardians above sandy beaches. He caught sight of the plantation home with its sweeping verandas. The old mansion nestled like a pink blossom among the greenery of the rain forest. He tensed as the itch intensified—a sure sign trouble was headed his way. Shoving the errant unease aside, he brought *Darlin* to a graceful landing on the water. With a smooth swoop, he turned the plane around and edged toward the dock. He cut the engines, allowing the plane to coast until it reached the wooden pier. A young man caught the wing hook and tied it off.

Jackson grabbed his gear along with his precious cooler of specialties from his bayou home and opened the cabin door. Brandon Falcon stood at the far end of the dock. A thousand scenarios ran through Jackson's mind. It wasn't unheard of for the team leader to meet him, but combined with the bad feeling he had, something was up.

"Hey, Cap." Jackson automatically used the former SEAL's moniker. "Why do I get the feeling you're not here because you're happy to see me?"

Brandon Favre came forward and slapped Jackson on the back. "Who wouldn't be happy to see that Cajun face of yours? Love the new paint."

Jackson studied Brandon's face, searching for a clue to his welcome. A picture of Brandon's very pregnant wife flashed into his mind. "What's up? Is Mira okay?"

He had a special fondness for 'Doc' as he called Brandon's wife. Isolated as they were on Coffee Island, her pregnancy was a major concern for the entire team because of the lack of a medical facility. Brandon worried that she would go into labor with no one around—hence his harried look.

Brandon got behind the wheel of the jeep. "She's fine, but she won't slow down."

Unease trickled down Jackson's back like cold sweat. Brandon had evaded his first question. He could count on one hand the times Cap had done that. All of them had meant trouble. He jumped into the passenger seat, and the jeep jerked forward. He took a deep breath both to calm his nerves and savor the familiar smells from the jungle.

They had only been on Coffee Island six months, yet the place felt like a favorite pair of jeans. A few silent moments passed before he turned and read the signs of fatigue, worry, and something dangerous on Brandon's face. His friend had aged considerably in the last year. Severely wounded during his mission to rescue Mira and find Rafa, Brandon was still recovering. He had gone out on a medical discharge and formed Brandon's Brigade.

"Tell me," Jackson growled. "What's wrong?"

The jeep slowed, pulled off the dirt track, and stopped in the shade of a papaya tree.

"Do you trust me, Jackson?" Brandon asked.

"Cap, you know I trust you with my life. What's got you in such a tailspin?" He waited expectantly. This behavior was so unlike the man whom he'd followed through the hells of Afghanistan and the jungles of Honduras.

"I have to go away for a few weeks. I'll be out of contact the entire time. You will be in charge while I'm gone." Brandon looked as if he had more to say but closed his mouth.

"*Maudit*, Cap!" Jackson cursed. "Have those pen-pushers in Washington tied you up in another op? Don't trust them."

"It's personal—something only I can do." Brandon looked away and then continued. "Rafa will take care of the training side. You're in charge of everything else, including my about-to-pop wife." A smile flashed across the gaunt face.

"She's going to birth that baby, pronto, when she finds out about this." Jackson didn't envy his friend that conversation. Mira had once nearly lost Brandon in the jungles of Honduras under the worst conditions imaginable. No way was she going to meekly accept Cap's disappearance this close to the baby coming. Besides, Doc didn't do meek.

Brandon shrugged. "That's the tricky part. She can't know anything about this. As far as she's concerned, I'm negotiating with the Navy for funding and more men." He restarted the jeep. "I don't want her upset or worried."

Jackson stalled. "Have you forgotten about the new equipment? I can't get that up and running while taking care of the rest." If his friend thought something was important enough to leave Mira in his hands in her condition, it was serious. Jackson would bend over backward to make sure everything went according to plan.

Brandon quickly faced forward and eased the jeep back on the track. "I managed to get you some tech help. The equipment arrived along with the technician while you were visiting your *grandmère*. All I ask is that you keep an open mind and cut her some slack. We're in for a lot of changes in the next few months."

Jackson grimaced as a hard knot tightened in his belly. Brandon was holding something back, and it worried him. He loved the man like a father but, prying information out of him was as easy as wrestling a gator. His tightened jaw would remain clamped shut until he was ready.

The jeep stopped in front of the sprawling porch where two women waited. Jackson jumped out and enveloped the blonde with the protruding belly in a bear hug. "*Cher*, you're glowing with beauty," he said in his smoothest voice.

They didn't call him the Cajun Prince for nothing. He loved all women. No matter the age, shape, or size, he'd spent most of his life practicing his charms on every female he met—much to his *grandmère's* chagrin.

Mira Falcon laughed and hugged him back. "I feel like a hippopotamus."

Jackson turned to the old nurse who now took care of the house for them. "Rosita, I brought groceries and have some Andouille and Boudin sausages." His accent thickened when he spoke of two of his favorite foods. "I've got some spices and a cookbook for you, too."

"If you've finished sweeping the women off their feet, let's get Mira in where it's cool." Brandon moved around Jackson and led his wife inside.

Jackson followed the women and Brandon through a large entryway alive with lush plants, into an enormous sitting room. At the back of the room, an elegant curving staircase led to a second-floor balcony. Numerous rooms opened off the balcony, each leading to a bedroom. His friend had worked furiously to complete the renovations to the old home before his wife joined him on the island. Unfortunately, the old homestead was still a work in progress. Getting the business up and running took priority over the house.

Jackson allowed Rosita to take the cooler from him. He moved toward the back of the house while the others went up to their rooms. The men had taken several smaller rooms on the ground floor and made them into offices. The outer office also served as their conference room. He pushed open the door and was met with a breathtaking sight—long feminine legs leading upward to a curvaceous bottom encased in snug shorts. With her back to him, she appeared to be concentrating on unpacking, so didn't notice his entrance. Each move she made tightened the fabric across her hips. His pulse quickened. This could prove interesting.

"Hello, *cher*. I'm Jackson Favre. Welcome to the team."

Her back stiffened, and she dropped what she had in her arms. She stood upright and slowly turned around.

Jackson had only a moment to catch his breath before he came face-to-face with his past. Here was the reason for his unease. Her glossy brown hair hung to her chin where it curled under and hugged her cheeks. That stubborn chin lifted into the air with challenge. Her eyes sparked blue fire and shadowed pain haunted their depths as she gave him a straightforward look. At five feet, nine inches, she was tall but still had to look up at him. His heart nearly stopped and then began to race frantically.

"Charlie! You're dead," he blurted. For the first time in his life, he felt faint. Anger quickly welled up and overshadowed his happiness at finding her alive. "Where have you been for the last three years?"

****

Charlene Bowman stared into the face that had haunted her for years. The same whiskey-brown eyes had turned her insides to mush when she'd been younger. But he had changed. Gone was the boyish Cajun who'd taken her breath away and stolen her heart. In his place stood a hard-edged man—rugged, dangerous. He still had the swarthy good looks and wavy black hair, but his body had filled out with toned-and-tight muscles. Something inside her stirred, and she dropped her gaze. God! He was potent.

"You look good, Jackson," she said coolly. Happy with her controlled words, she turned to finish unloading the specialized communications equipment Brandon had ordered. She couldn't face Jackson for long without getting emotional, and that was out of the question.

Brandon Falcon had offered her a chance to redeem herself and she intended to justify his trust. Getting involved with Jackson again would be a bad idea. No—it would be devastating. Her heart had been ripped from her once—but not again.

He moved closer. "*Bon Dieu, cher.*"

Her pulse raced as her chest tightened. Part of her ached to reach out and cling to him while the saner Charlene understood the danger. Fear, not for her safety, but for her peace of mind sent her searching for a place to run. Crossing her arms, she steadied her shaking hands and stepped around the box. She'd done enough running. Stiffening her spine, she looked up at his chin. If she avoided his eyes, she could do this.

"I know you want an explanation, but I just can't." Her voice pitched higher. "You deserve one. There's so much to say—"

He turned away, his fists clenched at his side. "Damned right there's a lot to say. What happened, Charlene? I thought we were good together."

"We were," she whispered to his back. "We were better than good."

"Then why leave without a word? You could have trusted me with anything." He turned back to her and pulled her into his arms.

"Stop, please," she pleaded.

Desperate, she fought her body's response to him. For three years she'd yearned for his nearness. Now, his touch sent sparks through her skin. He pulled her closer, hands kneading her back. His heady scent filled her with longing. She caught herself and reached way down for strength. "No!' She pushed him away. "I'm sorry I hurt you, Jackson, but I have a job to do here. It's important to me to make this work. One day soon we'll talk, but not now."

Charlene stepped back, putting distance between them. Her ragged breaths echoed in her ears. Inhaling deeply, she calmed herself. She had to make him understand.

Jackson snarled, his face a mask of contempt. "What the hell?"

"I mean"—she emphasized each word—"you're going to be my boss."

As if she had struck him, astonishment flashed across his face. After a moment he brightened. He gave her a devious look and flashed a grin.

Unease pooled in her belly, erasing the heat his embrace had triggered.

"*Laissez les bon temps rouler, cher*!" With a huge smirk on his face, Jackson Favre walked briskly from the room.

"Let the good times roll, my ass," she muttered to his back.

It was going to take every ounce of her courage to face him each day. Lord, she was in trouble. How had she allowed herself to be talked into this? Brandon Falcon could charm the panties off a nun. She was far from a nun, and now she had to figure out a way to work with Jackson, who was also a dangerous charmer.

Her spirits lifted a notch, and she left the room in search of the mouthwatering aromas coming from the kitchen.

****

Dinner was easier than she'd imagined. Jackson opted to dine with the men down at the bunkhouse. No doubt he was busy planning any number of ways to make her life hell. The look in his eyes before he'd thrown his taunt and walked away, spelled trouble. He wanted to strike out and hurt her as he'd been hurt. She understood his desire to do so, but she couldn't let him get to her.

"Charlene." Brandon called her name for the second time.

"What? Oh, forgive me. My mind was wandering."

Brandon took a corn muffin and passed the basket to Mira. "I'm sure you have lots to think about. Will this work between you and Jackson?"

"Give them some time. She's only been here two days." Mira gave Charlene an encouraging smile. "Jackson has a flare for the dramatic, but he's fair."

Charlene cringed. She felt like a specimen under a microscope. Isolated here on Café Caye, living in the same house with the man, would make privacy difficult. She'd known Brandon from other operations, but Mira and the other household members were new to her. She'd been cut off from all contact with the past while she sorted through the mess her life had become. It was time to start interacting with people and return to the land of the living.

"Don't worry, we'll make it work," Charlene assured her boss. She might answer directly to Jackson, but everyone answered to Brandon. She switched topics. "Will Rafa be back soon?"

Just then, the door opened, and Rafael Gutiérrez breezed in and joined them at the table.

"Speak of the devil." Brandon laughed.

"What did I miss?" Rafa leaned down to kiss Mira's cheek before sitting. "By the way, who put a burr up Jackson's—?" He fell silent at a scowl from Brandon and did a double take when he spotted Charlene.

Heat burned her cheeks. "Good to see you, Rafa." Clearly, Jackson wasn't the only one who hadn't known she was coming. She'd left that decision up to Brandon so couldn't complain.

"Charlie," Rafa mumbled the one word, then looked away as if uncomfortable.

"You've been out in the jungle too much. Things have changed fast around here." Mira's comment eased the tension.

The rest of the meal passed in congenial conversation with only the occasional comment from the men. As they rose to end the meal, Charlene made a beeline for her bedroom.

Brandon's voice caught her on the stairs. "Eight a.m. sharp."

She flashed a grin over her shoulder and fled for sanctuary. "Right, boss."

Chapter Two

The next morning Brandon focused on the unhappy face of the woman before him—his heart and soul. "You know I wouldn't go if I could solve this any other way," he whispered huskily. Damn, it was hard to argue when she looked as if she might drop his baby at any minute—and the crocodile tears. His gut twisted into a knot the size of a pineapple.

Mira looked at him with accusation in her eyes. "You promised, no more secret government missions." Her breath came out in gasps. "You've done your part for God and country and nearly died doing it. The baby and I need you."

Guilt tore at him. He pulled her into his arms, and her breasts pressed snugly against his chest. Sharply, he inhaled her scent and pressed her closer, memorizing the feel of her in his arms. He ran his hands down her back, then cupped her face with the gentlest of touches. "Shh. Don't make this harder for me than it already is."

He eased back when she pushed on his chest. "The baby is due in a few weeks. Is this mission important enough to miss the birth of our child?"

He *had* promised her he wouldn't go back to the dangerous job he had as a SEAL, and he never went back on his word. This job, *he'd* volunteered to take, and she couldn't know the purpose. Her uncle Max, her only family, had been located. He worked for the CIA and had been missing for the past two years. Brandon was going to Russia to extract him. "Nothing is more important to me, but sometimes circumstances make it impossible to do as you wish."

She moved to the dresser and ran her fingers lightly over the small treasures displayed on the top. "There's nothing I can do to change your mind, is there?" Her voice was resigned but no longer accusing.

"No, I'm committed."

She turned back to him and splayed her palms across his chest. "Promise me you'll do everything in your power to come back to me, safe and sound."

He pulled her tightly against him, impressing the feel of her body into his soul. "Always, my love." Her tears dampened his shirt. "Don't, you know what your tears do to me." He tilted her head and kissed the salty drops. "Shh, everything will be fine."

"When do you leave?"

"In two days. I'm meeting with the team in a few minutes to discuss our plans for my absence." Something thumped his abdomen.

Mira laughed. "Our baby might have something to say about this."

Brandon caressed her swollen belly and received another kick for his efforts. Dropping a kiss where the hard lump of a foot pushed outward, he then kissed Mira's forehead and stepped back. "Make sure you don't overdo," he admonished and walked from the room.

****

Brandon left the bedroom with heavy steps and headed for the office. He would ache all day for the pain he'd caused her. Keeping the reason behind this mission a secret from her wasn't his choice, but he couldn't compromise the others involved. He had a lot to do before he left. First, he had to get his team organized. He was entrusting them with the care of Mira and his baby—they had to be prepared. Opening the door to the office, he met three inquiring faces. They were all curious. He'd only given limited information to Jackson. Rafa and Charlene were in the dark.

Rafa rose from his seat and poured a cup of coffee from the carafe. "Morning, Cap." He handed the cup to Brandon and sat back down.

"Good morning, everyone." Brandon paused to take a sip of coffee. As always, he relished the flavor of the special blend. "We have a lot to do and only two days to prepare. I'm leaving for a special mission."

Charlene gave him a startled look. "But Mira is so close to having the baby."

"I know. I told her about the mission a few minutes ago. She's very upset and will need everyone's help to get through this. I'm counting on you, Charlene, to be her friend."

"I'll do everything I can to make it easier for her," she said.

"Good. Let's get down to business." He pulled out the chair at the head of the table and sat. "Rafa, how are things going at the camp?"

"Fine, except we're a little shorthanded. It's a good thing we have more people joining us. They should arrive within the week."

"As soon as they get here, train them fast and hard. I'd like to think we're ready for anything." He turned to Jackson. "You'll oversee Brandon's Brigade while I'm gone. It's a big responsibility, but one I think you're more than capable of doing."

Jackson sat up a little straighter. “I’ll do my best.”

“Rafa, explain to Charlene what our Brigade is all about.”

Rafa unfolded a map and tacked it to the bulletin board. He grabbed a pointer and indicated a large orange rectangle on the northwestern side of Coffee Island. “This is the training camp. It’s where we train elite military teams in jungle tactics. We’re basically a subcontractor for the armed forces. Washington calls the shots on who we train; we call the shots on how they’re trained.”

Charlene stopped toying with her pen. “I didn’t realize we were working so closely with the military. Are we under their control?”

“No,” Jackson answered before Rafa could open his mouth. “We get funding and equipment from them along with a set paycheck per unit we train. We also test new equipment and weapons for them.”

Brandon caught her gaze and smiled. “We’re not a government puppet. I worked very hard to set the guidelines, so we’d have as much autonomy as possible. We are working to develop an elite extraction team, specializing in the rescue of kidnap victims.”

“Isn’t that what the SEALs do?” Charlene blurted.

Brandon heard the concern in her voice. She’d been burned badly after she separated from the elite eight-week training program. “Yes, they do, but there are situations where they’re not allowed to deploy. For instance, they can’t operate within the Continental US. Only the FBI can handle those cases. There are times when someone is taken and not important enough for the U.S. Government to intervene. We get paid to go in and rescue them.”

Charlene met his gaze briefly, then lowered her gaze to her fingers. "And that involves lots of money?"

Her words carried a tone of accusation; he took a breath before continuing. "Don't go painting us as mercenaries. We run a business and get paid well to do what we do. Those who have money get a chance at freedom. It isn't fair, but it's reality."

Rafa tapped the map with his pointer, bringing everyone's attention back to the display board. "The camp is where we house and train the soldiers. Designated Beta-zone, it's secured behind gates with armed guards and high electric fences. No one enters or leaves this area without permission."

He moved the pointer to the other end of the island. "This yellow strip is a small native village. We call this area CP-zone for Civilian Population. Though we own the island, they've been here for generations. We leave them alone, except when someone needs help. Doc goes down once a week to look after their medical needs."

"You own the island?" Charlene stared at Brandon. "How the hell did you pull that off?"

"Don't get your hackles up. It's all legit. This island was confiscated from drug dealers. In a special exit package, the team and I got the island—as long as we trained soldiers for at least five years. After that, it's ours outright."

Charlene looked somewhat mollified but still concerned. "I assume the blue area is the homestead?"

"Right," Rafa said and continued. "The homestead has the designation Alpha-zone. Brandon is Alpha-one, Jackson is Alpha-two and Rafa is Alpha-three. It's very important not to use proper names over the radio. Most of your time will be spent here at the house." He moved the pointer to a small green area adjacent to the blue rectangle. "This is Mira's research area. We call it Spider-zone after the orchid she's researching."

Brandon interrupted. "Charlene, I need you to research the security setup and improve it as much as you can. Besides housing the priceless orchids and research, I worry about Mira's safety. She's isolated there."

Rafa wasn't finished. "Everything in white is safe to travel, but avoid the jungle, which is called Camo-zone, and marked in purple. The men will be using live ammo in their training."

"How is the management of the Brigade set up?" Charlene asked.

"The three of us are equal partners." Brandon said. "We equally share the workload and the profits." He met the gazes of his partners. "We've fought together and are brothers." He cleared his throat of the emotion clogging it before continuing. "We each have different jobs but can handle any part of the operation. I do most of the paperwork and administrative duties."

Charlene butted in. "So you're the one I have to thank for the mess in here?"

He laughed. "Guilty as charged, but I've had a little help." He eyed the boxes and stacks of unorganized papers. Charlene was going to be a godsend. "Rafa oversees the training camp and goes on missions. Jackson flies the plane or copter on missions or business. He also helps with the training.

Charlene leaned forward. "What does my job entail?"

"Everything from the usual clerical duties, setting up communications and organizing the administrative side of the team."

He seemed to find her shock funny. He'd already asked her to be Mira's personal bodyguard. The job was daunting, but he believed she could handle it. If she and Jackson could work together, maybe there could be some healing—but that was the second part of his plan.

****

"You can't be serious," Charlene sputtered.

How the hell was she going to manage everything Brandon had laid out? Not to mention protecting Mira and checking the security setup. When he approached her with this job, she'd been torn. It was what she'd dreamed of doing, yet she and Jackson had a past—and she had secrets. The thought sent a frisson of unease down her spine. The man she fell in love with had been young and immature. In the three years they'd been apart, he'd grown and changed. The new Jackson was a man who looked like he'd had seen and done things best forgotten. Hard edginess marked his face, and bulky musculature hardened his tall body—all hidden behind whisky eyes and Cajun charm.

"You'll be fine." Brandon's voice brought her reverie to a screeching halt. Her ink pen fell from slack fingers as she scrambled to assess what she might have missed.

When no one said a word, he ended with, "Good, let's get to it."

The three men left Charlene alone in the chaos of her new office. Her gaze slid over the stack of new equipment and taller stack of unsorted papers. She heaved a deep sigh. All three members of Brandon's Brigade could disarm nuclear weapons or extract hostages from impossible situations, but could they manage to put a letter or receipt in a file folder?

She wasn't here to be a secretary, though that would be her role when outsiders were around. She was trained in security and could outshoot Brandon, who was a trained sniper. She couldn't complain, though. This work drew her like a magnet. She'd take it one day at a time and let the "thing" between her and Jackson coast. Digging through the cabinet, she found folders and attacked the boxes spilling over with paperwork. Her organization of Brandon's Brigade began.

Her temples throbbed after only an hour of sorting. The move, meeting Jackson again, and the enormity of her job responsibilities made her headache worse. She couldn't do everything at once. Charlene stood from her seat on the floor and stretched her shoulders and back. The tempting smell of coffee drifted to her nostrils, dampening all thoughts of paperwork. She followed her nose and ended up in the kitchen.

As she entered, Rosita bustled over to her with a steaming coffee mug in her hand. "Sit, *Señorita* Bowman. It's time you took a break from that room they call an office. Those men let things stay where they were dropped."

Charlene sat at the kitchen table that was adorned with a vase of exotic blooms. As she took her first sip of the delightful brew, Rosita set a plate of fresh-baked sticky buns on the table beside her. Her mouth watered. She grabbed a plate and quickly slid one of the buns onto it. "Rosita, please tell me you cook these often."

"*Si, Señorita* Bowman. I love to bake."

"Call me Charlene, please. I plan on being a regular at this table at break time."

Rosita laughed and wiped her hands on the towel at her waist. "The three *señors* are big eaters. I always have something ready because of their unusual schedules.

Mira walked in and headed straight for the sticky buns. Her eyes were shadowed, the area around them red and puffy. "I don't think calories count at this stage. "I feel like a whale."

Charlene's heart turned over for the other woman. She admired her spirit, though. Brandon hadn't come out of that meeting unscathed. His eyes had shown sadness before he'd gathered himself and slipped his boss persona into place. "Nonsense, you're absolutely glowing." She got up to refill her cup. "Have you two discussed names yet?"

Mira brightened. "We've decided on Maxine if it's a girl and Justin if it's a boy. I'm so excited." Her smile faded and the light left her face. "I just hope Brandon gets back in time for the birth."

Charlene decided to work at putting that glow back. Mira was passionate about her work, so she began there. "What kind of work are you doing on the exotic plant you discovered?"

"Actually, Rafa found it. I'd been searching for years, but he found it by accident when he was stranded on a mission. I had to use the one specimen he found in order to save Brandon's life. I thought the Blue Spider Orchid and its mysterious healing powers would be lost forever, but Rafa went back and found a couple more."

"How exciting. Are you trying to extract whatever makes it miraculous? Brandon asked me to check out the security in the research lab."

Mira's expression brightened. "You'll need a tour to really understand it all. Any research of this type requires tight security. The plant is so rare, people might be tempted to steal it for their own research. That's why I've kept the discovery as low-key as possible." She reached for another sticky bun, then slapped her own hand.

Charlene pushed her own plate aside and stood. "Do you feel up to giving me a look now? I'm tired of sorting paperwork and making some sense of the guys' personal filing techniques."

Mira laughed. "What filing method would that be? I have to be *so* careful with my research data. I'm a fanatic about everything in its place in the lab. Come on, I'll show you around."

"Let me get my notebook so I can jot things down. I'll meet you on the porch in a few minutes."

"That'll give me one more bathroom break before work. I swear this baby is dancing on my bladder. Count yourself lucky you don't have this problem."

Charlene felt a stab of pain at the words She knew it didn't matter—no one knew her past and couldn't be expected to be careful of her feelings. Breathing deeply, she let the air out slowly. Over the past few years, she'd learned a great deal about finding calm. Shaking her head, she entered her room and grabbed her notepad.

About to leave, she remembered her main job—as Mira's bodyguard. With steady hands, she opened the footlocker and looked at her guns. In this climate, there was no way of hiding the gun with clothing. After some deliberation, she chose the little snub-nosed Glock and the back holster. She strapped on the holster and slid the gun home. With haste, she untucked her shirt and looked in the mirror. Happy it could only be seen by a trained eye, she headed for the porch.

Mira sat behind the wheel of the ATV like she belonged. Granted, there was little room between her and the wheel, but she looked ready to face anything.

Charlene laughed and climbed in beside her host. "I didn't know we were going on safari."

"Brandon and the guys insist I have a vehicle with me at all times. It's not a long distance, but currently, I appreciate the wheels."

They took off over the well-maintained track, giving Charlene time to absorb the vibrant-green colors and delightful smells.

Mira slowed for a bump and glanced at her. "You never get used to it. The colors—the smells. I love the breeze scented by the sea."

"In my second lifetime, maybe. Right now, I'm enjoying the novelty." Charlene took note of the distance they'd traveled from the house. Mira's lab was really isolated here—not good for security. "Are you alone out here when you work?"

"For now. It's an island and has three ex-Navy SEALs and soldiers crawling through the jungle. I get qualms sometimes, but I worry *more* about the safety of the research rather than myself."

As they approached the building, Charlene studied the building with critical eyes. It would take a lot of time to completely secure Mira's research facility, but video monitoring was a priority. And a fence. The building and the surrounding area needed to be secured from anyone who might risk coming to the island. There was a tree too close to the building. It would make accessing the roof far too easy.

Mira parked under the tree, and they both got out. Charlene turned in a circle, surveying the area. The house couldn't be seen from here. They either needed a direct line of sight to the house or twenty-four-hour night-vision cameras. As security conscious as Brandon was, she was surprised he hadn't already added it. Of course, he had his hands full with getting the company up and running. She was happy she could take this worry off his mind.

Mira unlocked the door with a simple key, and they stepped into a mud room. Slots for boots and hooks with lab jackets lined the wall. Above these, short lockers provided room for wallets or personal items. She paused, jotting down the need for a coded lock and a better door. This place had obviously been set up quickly to meet the basic needs for research.

She gazed around at the shallow cabinets and cubicles, silently calculating the square footage. "This looks like you're planning for some help in the future."

Mira paused to slip off her sandals and slide her feet into clogs. "I'm the only person, for the time being. Miguel, Ana's husband, helps with the heavy stuff, and I do the rest. Ana normally helps at the homestead, but they needed her at the men's cafeteria. I'd like to train her to help eventually, but she's needed at the camp for the time being."

"Who will take care of the plants and keep the records when the baby comes?"

Mira looked uncomfortable. "I need an assistant, but it's hard with camp security and the need for secrecy with the research. We've been trying not to advertise our current operation, so finding someone to help will be difficult."

"I think it should be a priority. Before Brandon leaves, we need to have help for you lined up. What kind of person are you looking for?"

"That's the hard part. I need a trained researcher—with at least a master's degree and research experience."

Mira opened the inner door, and they stepped into a prep room. Planting supplies and research materials lined shelves labeled neatly with plastic tags.

Charlene admired the tidiness of the area as they turned left and walked down a short hall. Ahead of them stood a steel-enclosed room with a coded lock on the door. Now, this was more like it. She didn't have to ask what was behind these doors. Mira would only have such security around the most precious part of the lab. This is where the Blue Spider Orchid would be.

Mira stepped up and keyed in the code. The door clicked, and she turned the handle. Bright, fluorescent lighting and the smell of earth and moisture greeted them. Sliding back another panel, Mira revealed the reason for all the fuss. Vivid-blue petals grew in clusters along a very flimsy-looking stem. The flower looked delicate, until you noticed the hairy petal extensions, that vaguely looked like a yellow-and-black spider. Well, it was aptly named.

"What do you think?" Her face, reflected in the glass panels, glowed with pride.

Charlene laughed. "I think you're a remarkable woman, and I envy your brain."

"There's nothing wrong with yours. It's just wired on a different wavelength." Mira ushered her out and re-keyed the code to lock the door. "One more place to see before we head to my office. Rosita always keeps it stocked with fresh lemonade and food for my munchies."

They went back down the hall and opened another door which led into the greenhouse. As they passed through the plastic strips used for temperature control, sticky heat engulfed them. Here, rows of flats containing tiny plants lined planting tables. She bent down, hoping for a closer look. She discovered each plant had its own letter and numerical designation. Detail. She once more appreciated Mira's dedication.

"You did all this by yourself?"

"I just planted them. Miguel did the hard stuff." She gently touched a tiny seedling. "Each plant must be examined daily, misted, and the data carefully recorded in a logbook. Twice a week, I put all data into the computer and back it up in three different places."

Charlene jotted a note in her book. The logbook was vulnerable. Figure out a better way. "Where do you keep the logbook?"

Mira hesitated and then looked at her with leery eyes. "You have to understand. No one knows where I keep it."

Charlene noted the tense shoulders and tightened lips of her host. "You don't trust me?"

"I've trusted before and nearly died as a result. My husband is the only one I trust completely."

Charlene absorbed the statement, giving her the chance to come up with the right words. She needed this woman's complete trust, or any chance for keeping her safe were zero. "I'm going to tell you something about your husband."

Mira nodded and said simply, "Okay."

After letting out a deep cleansing breath, Charlene said, "I didn't apply for this job. I've been in hiding for three years. Brandon sought me out to come here. I trusted him to keep my secrets, and he trusted me to help the love of his life."

Mira gasped. "What secrets?"

Charlene winced. She wasn't prepared to dredge up her past—especially since it was catching up to her. "I can't talk about it. Like you, I have trust issues. Let's just say, I have no desire to steal your plants or research. I'm here to make you safe, especially when Brandon leaves."

"I see. I suppose if he trusts you that much, I can trust you to keep my data secure. I photograph each log entry with my phone, then hide the logbook in the vault with the mature orchids."

Charlene jotted this down, then looked at Mira. "I see several ways that could compromise your work. I'll work on some details and talk to you about implementing them. Is there anywhere I haven't seen?"

"Yes, my office-and-lab combo. I'm the only one allowed in there. It's a work in progress, and I still need more equipment. That will have to wait until after the baby comes. I can only spread myself so far." Mira grabbed the edge of one of the tables and took her weight off her right leg.

"You need to sit. Show me the office, and I'll take some notes while you sit and sip some lemonade. Deal?"

"Deal. This way." Mira headed back to the door.

They returned to the hallway leading to the vault. She hadn't noticed the door to the right of the vault, but there it was, tucked away from view of the casual observer. Once more Mira keyed in a code and opened the door to her office.

Mira waved her hand around. "Here is where all the research is done."

"Nice setup. You're the only one with the code?"

"Yes, but that will have to change when I get an assistant. For now, if someone needs me, they call on the walkie-talkie, and I go out to meet them."

Charlene saw no evidence of said device on Mira's person. "Where is your walkie-talkie? I hope it isn't the only way you have of contacting the house or camp."

Mira gave her a sheepish look. "I guess I forgot it. I do have a wall set here by my desk." She pointed out the set attached to the wall. "I just realized, no one would know if something was wrong—if something happened to me. The door automatically locks and there are no windows."

"Exactly. Your isolation and your need for secrecy are putting you at physical risk. I'll need to devise some sort of emergency alarm. I'm really worried about your safety. Where's that lemonade you promised me? I'll check out the lab and office space while you put your feet up."

Mira rolled her cushy desk chair to the table and sat. "In the fridge beside the coffee bar. The glasses are in the cabinet above."

"Put your feet up; I've got this."

Charlene grabbed two glasses, set them on the counter, and opened the fridge. Mira hadn't been kidding. The refrigerator was packed with food and drink. Something niggled at the edge of her brain. She grabbed the pitcher of lemonade and a small tray of finger sandwiches. After filling the glasses, she brought them to the table, then got the sandwiches.

"Here we go." She sat down at the table and took a bite of a chicken salad sandwich. "How does Rosita get in to stock the fridge?

She either comes with me or sends it with Miguel or Brandon. He's determined to keep me hydrated and fed." Mira watched her, a serious expression clouding her usually happy face. "How much do you know about babies?"

Charlene nearly choked on the food in her mouth.

Her gaze flew to Mira's, and she recognized a sly look. Uneasy, she grabbed her drink and washed down the suddenly huge bite. *My God. Had Brandon told her*? No, he'd promised, and he kept his promises.

"What do you mean?"

"Just wondering, you have a maternal look about you."

"Must be my hips. I've always thought they were too wide." Charlene made light of the question and Mira's comment about her maternal look. The question and comment were far too close to the truth.

The ride back to the house was completed in silence. Charlene shoved the disturbing question to the back of her mind. Instead, she jotted down more notes about what she had seen. This part of her job would be a major undertaking. She'd have to put together a plan and work out the details with Mira and the team.

Chapter Three

As Jackson stood on the veranda, his eyes narrowed when the ATV pulled to a stop. He rushed to help Mira from the jeep, but she shook her head and wiggled out of the seat. She might think herself unattractive, but the full bloom of motherhood brought a glow to skin, hair, and eyes. His gaze swerved to Charlene, and he couldn't miss the look of longing on her face. Something inside stirred. "How was the tour?"

"Great," Mira said. "I think Charlene is going to be a great asset to the team. She already has some ideas for beefing up security at the lab. I'm impressed with her quick observations. You'd think she was a closet scientist."

"Is she, now?"

Jackson wasn't sure what she was anymore. He'd thought he'd known Charlie as well as any man could know a woman. She could fight as well as any soldier and was a prize-winning sharpshooter. Her computer skills surpassed anyone's on the team. Obviously, she had beefed up her technology and training since they'd been together.

His mind shied away from the memories those thoughts stirred up.

Grasping for something to blot the pain, he recalled a picture of her petting a baby gazelle at the Virginia State Zoo. Her eyes had softened as she cooed sweet words to the animal. He'd teased her about it when they got home.

"Jackson?" Charlene spoke his name now.

He turned at the sound of his name. "Are you ready for our tour of the island? It's pretty extensive, so if you need a break, I'll understand." He waited for her to grab at the excuse he offered. As much as she might need to get her bearings, he wasn't in the mood to spend all day in her company. There was too much between them to spend any length of time together.

"No, I'm fine. Will these clothes work, or do I need to change?"

"You might want to change into hiking boots. You can bring your swimsuit if you like; we'll cool off before the trip home."

She gave him a sharp look before nodding her assent and stepping down from the jeep. "I'll be right back."

Twenty minutes later, the jeep lunged through an especially deep rut, throwing Charlene against his shoulder. With all senses on high alert, Jackson felt her stiffen, then pull back. Pain vibrated in his heart. How could she react to him as if he was some stranger with devious motives? They'd been best friends. His life went to hell after she disappeared.

He couldn't stop the harsh words spilling from his mouth. "What the hell are you afraid of, Charlene? Dammit, we were lovers. Not once did I hurt you—physically or otherwise."

"I'm afraid these ruts are going to throw me into your lap," she shouted over the noise of the jeep. "I'm not afraid of you. I'm just not ready to hand out explanations. I've only got two days to gather as much information as possible before Brandon leaves, so stop being so touchy."

Her words acted like ice water, dousing the flames of anger he'd held in since she'd reappeared out of the blue. "I'm sorry, *cher*. I'm stressed right now. I shouldn't have jumped on you." Her response made him feel like a bully. Their relationship before had never contained anything like that. "Shall we call a truce? The day is far too beautiful to be cranky."

As he waited for her answer, he slowed the jeep. They were approaching the little wetland which separated the rain forest from the beach. He pulled to the side of the track and stopped.

Charlene swung her head in his direction. "Why are we stopping?"

"This is one of my favorite spots on the island. Freshwater runs from the forest, but it turns brackish when it approaches the sea. You can see all kinds of birds here. One of my favorites is the scarlet ibis. Look—there's one on the far side of those reeds."

"I never knew you were a bird watcher."

"I've had some time to ponder life since I saw you last. I decided to catch all the good there is to see. God knows, there's too much evil."

Charlene twisted round to face him. "You've had to kill since we were together, haven't you?"

"I've had to do things that twist me up inside. I keep those images locked away."

He inhaled the smell of the water as the breeze blew in their direction. Her hair blew around her face, and she reached up to brush it back behind her ears. Their eyes met, and awareness flared between them. Her eyes dilated, and her lips parted slightly—invitingly. He couldn't help himself. Moving slowly, his gaze never leaving hers, he leaned over and covered her lips with his own. Her breath hitched and her mouth softened. Flashes of desire sent a jolt southward beneath his jeans.

****

Charlene abruptly pulled back. Her ragged breaths sounded like a sputtering steam engine between them. Sensation swamped her, dredging up feelings she'd thought long buried. What was it about this man that drew her to him? She always felt his presence as soon as he entered a room. In the close confines of the jeep, that feeling filled her with panic. How could she have forgotten? No way could she indulge herself. She had responsibilities; greater than any short-term gratification she might get from giving in—allowing him to take control. "No, we can't do this."

Jackson pulled back. "Why the hell not? We're both old enough to know what we want."

She turned to look at the small, serene lagoon. Why couldn't her life be as peaceful as this idyllic scene? "It isn't about wanting." Her breathing slowed, and her voice hardened. "I'm here to do a job. Getting involved again would interfere with my responsibilities. You know the stakes. Brandon is counting on us to keep things running and Mira safe."

He jerked around. "I could almost hate you for all the pain you've caused me. The hell of it is, I don't."

His words sent shafts of pain to her heart. She deserved it—had left him with no explanation. God, this was a mess. She shook her head and grabbed the grip bar as Jackson started up the jeep and stepped on the gas. It jerked forward. So much for viewing the scenery. The landscape flew by as they careened along the track toward the camp.

Chapter Four

Careful to keep her expression bland while her pulse raced, Charlene stared back at him. Why did he insist they take this tour of the island alone? She wasn't afraid of him. Truth be told, she was afraid of herself. When faced with a handsome Jackson Favre, half-naked on a beach, how long would her control last? It would be crazy to tempt herself—but she would. She turned her face up and met his gaze with a steady one of her own. "I'm game if you are."

He nodded and sped up. "Let's get started."

Charlene relaxed back into the seat and decided to enjoy herself. "What's next?"

"The village." Jackson shifted gears. "We'll only have time for a quick drive-through. Prepare yourself, it was nearly wiped out in Hurricane Peter last year. Most of the villagers were lucky to get out with their lives."

Charlene felt the pang of loss for the people. She never had money in her own life, but these people had next to nothing. "Couldn't we help them somehow?"

"We do what we can, but they are a proud people whose deep-rooted independence only allows the most basic aid."

"Tell me some of the history of the village."

"Rafa's the local expert. With his Mexican ancestry, he developed an interest and did some research. Most of the villagers are a mix of Creole and Mayan. They are descended from the Baymen slaveholders and slaves brought from Africa for the logging industry. They're religious—nearly all Christian with a few of the more-exotic varieties. You'll get to check it out when Mira goes in for what she calls a health day."

"How often?" Charlie asked.

"Once a week, unless she's needed for an emergency."

The track rose gradually as they headed toward the mountainous part of the island. There was no official road around the perimeter of the island, only rough tracks used for centuries by donkey-drawn carts.

He turned the jeep onto an even rougher trail. Bushes brushed the vehicle as they bounced along the rocky track. This one sloped downward as they headed toward the coast again. A patchwork of huts sprang out of the weeds, becoming more numerous as the track widened into a central area surrounded by small houses on stilts.

Through the trees she caught glimpses of blue water. Dodging ragged children who flocked to the jeep, they continued through the village, emerging from the trees onto a beautiful shoreline. Boats of all shapes and sizes were tied to a rickety dock. The dock crossed the rocky outcrop until it reached aquamarine-blue water. Fishermen dragged nets as children used the makeshift diving platform to jump into the sea.

"How can this beauty exist next to such poverty? It doesn't seem possible," Charlene murmured.

"I don't know, *cher*, but it does. Let's move on. I'm sure you'll come back with Mira."

"Surely she won't go into that poverty with the baby so close."

Jackson laughed. "I'd like to see you stop her. The Doc has a very strong will. We'll try to stop her, of course, but she'll have her way in the end. She's an entity to be reckoned with."

The jeep gained speed, finally turning into a little cove complete with crystal-clear water and palm trees. Charlene jumped from the jeep before he could go around to help her.

****

"Damn," he uttered beneath his breath. Was she always going to be so skittish? He swallowed his irritation and flashed her his melt-your-bones grin. "Let's have some fun, *cher*."

Charlene ran for the sand, dropping to tug off her boots. "Last one in cleans up the picnic."

He relished the challenge. Charlie had always been competitive. Races to the shower, fastest to break down a gun and put it back together—all attached to some form of payment. Most of the time the contest ended in bed, both equals. He had always lost to her at the shooting range. She was the best of the best when it came to hitting a target. And oh, the payment she demanded.

Charlene giggled. "What's the holdup? I never knew you to daydream during a challenge."

Her words spurred him into action. His job required lots of quick changes. "A lady deserves a little head start."

The taunt worked. He laughed when she threw a handful of sand his way and shucked his clothes with speed born from years of practice. His muscled legs ate up the distance to the water, passing her as she struggled with her pant leg.

"Oomph." Jackson's world tilted, and he hit the

sand. What the hell? The splash of water drew his gaze. Mesmerized, he watched Charlene run into the sea. Her body had matured—more curvaceous. She still had the well-toned body of the woman he'd known, but her hips were wider, her breasts more bountiful.

She laughed back at him and dove into the water. "I thought Navy SEALs were a lot harder to put on the ground."

Jumping to his feet he ran the last few feet and dove in after her. Beneath the crystal-clear water, he was treated to a close-up view of her body as she swam. The black one-piece clung snugly to her curves as her firm body cut through the water with powerful strokes. She'd gone through training as tough as his—yet that was three years ago. Wherever she'd been, she'd kept in shape. He reached up and grabbed her ankle. Instead of stopping and sputtering her anger, she kicked back and pushed ahead to avoid his touch. Time to put an end to all her reticence. Trained to swim fast and long, he overtook her in seconds. Grabbing her around the chest, he stopped her momentum and pulled her up against him while he treaded water.

"You didn't play fair," he whispered into the supercharged atmosphere between them. They were quite a way from the shore, blue sky above and azure sea below. It was one of those special moments when time seemed to stand still. The light was like what the great masters expounded upon. It flickered, producing patterns of sparkling diamonds; she leaned in to claim his lips.

Cezanne and Picasso be dammed. This was real, and he intended to enjoy every second. He kicked to keep them afloat as she leaned in, placing her weight on his body. He hardened in response and ran his left hand down her back, then lower, cupping her buttocks. She softened against him. He drank in her sweetness. God, he'd missed this.

"Eek," she screeched, breaking the kiss and his hold on her.

"What the hell?" He swiftly surveyed the water around them then turned her to the left. A few yards away a large sea turtle swam in a lazy circle.

"I thought I was shark fodder." She laughed. "Is it safe to snorkel on the reef?"

"Yes, but it's best to take out one of the small boats. You don't want to get stuck out there if you have an accident. We'll take a break later in the week and go out. Now, it's time to swim back and have some food. Don't forget I told Rosita not to wait supper for us."

"I hadn't realized until you mentioned it. I'm starved." Splashing water in his face to give herself an advantage, she sped toward the shore with powerful strokes.

****

Charlene lost the race and breathed heavily as she stood on the wet sand. Jackson headed back from the jeep with a blanket and basket in hand. "I suppose I never stood a chance of winning."

He placed the basket on the sand and unfolded the blanket. "Nope."

She watched as he made another trip to the jeep, returning with a cooler and a couple of towels. He walked with an easy and precise stride. His body was hard and muscled. Her gaze swept the length of him, returning to his face. His eyes blazed with something she recognized from the past—desire, need, and intent. Something quivered in her lower body. The feeling frightened her. She hadn't felt anything sexual since… Fear rose to engulf her. With tremendous effort, she blocked the image.

Jackson dropped the cooler and towels. "What's wrong, *cher*?"

When he reached to touch her, she jerked back as if dodging a striking snake. Her body trembled, and her chest tightened. *Dammit, how can I kiss him one minute and panic at his touch the next?* Her mind struggled, confused by the dichotomy of conflicting emotions. The stir of desire she felt for him triggered memories she'd tried to bury.

After three years of counseling, she still couldn't control the panic when it hit like a brick in the face. Vivid flashes threatened to overwhelm her. She sank to her knees on the blanket. A towel plopped around her shoulders.

"Charlie, what is it? The expression on your face scares me. I've seen it many times in my work, but never on you. Why are you afraid of me?"

Strong arms—grabbing her from behind, cuffing her on the side of the head.

Charlene closed her eyes and breathed in through her nose and out through her mouth. Most times, the coping mechanism worked. How was she supposed to tell him it wasn't him she was afraid of…

But someone else.

Chapter Five

"Charlie, come back."

The command in Jackson's voice released Charlene from the hold the flashback had on her. "I'm here."

She grabbed the diet soda he handed her and drank deeply. A tiny niggle of feminine pride was happy to see he'd remembered her dislike of beer. He gazed at her with concern—the predatory look gone. The tightness in her chest eased. "I'm not afraid of you. I—"

"Eat. It can wait."

He'd set out the picnic food while she'd been in the past. She grabbed a piece of chicken, added some potato salad, and topped it with a handful of cherry tomatoes. She popped one of the red fruits into her mouth. "Are you happy here?"

Jackson set the chicken he'd been eating on the paper plate, evading her question with one of his own. "Is anyone ever truly happy?"

"Why did I know you weren't going to answer me?"

"You must have a touch of the *mojo*." As he always did, he laughed at the glare she'd sent him. "I suppose I'm as happy as most men like me. Brandon has given me the opportunity to be a part of something special. Ex-SEALs don't exactly slide smooth as glass back into society. The training, killing, and flashbacks make us a dangerous lot. Here, I can be myself without fear of hurting someone."

Charlene absorbed what he'd said. Jackson had been more forthcoming than she'd expected. Though they had worked together in the special program for civilians, he had always kept his darker side hidden beneath a flirtatious Cajun persona. While they ate in silence, she used the opportunity to collect herself as well as examine what he'd told her.

The way he'd spoken, she was certain he'd found his niche. For years, she'd thought he wanted a military career, which was why she'd sacrificed their relationship three years ago.

The long tour and the arduous swim caught up to her. "Would you be terribly upset if I snagged a nap?"

"I've got an umbrella in the jeep. You'll need to slather yourself in sunscreen. The breeze makes the sun's rays feel deceptively innocuous. We can't have you looking like a crawdad—red and ready to eat." He grabbed the umbrella, set it up, then handed her a tube of spf-50 sunscreen. "While you're napping, I'll go for a run. I missed training this morning."

He sat on the sand and tugged on a pair of sneakers. "If you wake up and want to cool off, feel free to swim in the shallow part of the water. We don't want any sharks having a late lunch."

"Thanks."

"For what?"

"For not pushing. I'm not ready."

She slipped on her sunglasses and grabbed the sunscreen as he stretched his leg muscles. He gave her a cocky grin and ran toward the beach. She lay back on the blanket and closed her eyes. Visions of his dark eyes flooded her consciousness. She shouldn't have given in to the urge to taste him. The kiss was just that—a kiss.

No need to read so much into it. Then why did she feel guilty? He'd been nothing but honest with her, and his lips had felt like heaven. She couldn't in good conscience renew their relationship with the shadow of her past looming like a thundercloud over her. She had to figure out a way to tell him the whole truth.

Charlene woke to a chill breeze on her sunbaked skin. The sun's rays burst onto the horizon in a showy splash of reds and oranges. A tinge of hot yellow near the sun's center made for a brilliant contrast. Jackson, back to her, sat on the sand by the water.

"It's beautiful," she murmured, wishing she was artistic and could capture the idyllic scene. He shifted, and his bronzed and scarred back turned away, changing the sight his powerful body made against the backdrop of sea, sand, and sky.

"I never get used to it. No matter how bad a mission has been or life generally kicking me in the ass—this renews me."

"I remember that about you. The sea or the bayou always held a siren's call for you."

"You slept a long time. Would you like to go for a walk?"

His enticing words had her up and grabbing her shirt. "Don't you get tired of all the exercise?"

He laughed and grabbed a beer and a soda from the cooler. "It's not exercise to me. It's a part of me, like breathing."

They set off down the beach, walking near each other but not touching. She moved closer to the water, bending to pick up small shells as they washed in on the turning tide. Growing up in central Georgia, she hadn't had many opportunities to visit the ocean. She especially loved the shells. The feel of her toes sucking into the wet sand as the water retreated, the call of the birds, and watching the little pipers look for food fascinated her. She couldn't believe she was here and would possibly live here. The thought brought her pause.

Before she could seriously consider the possibility, she'd have to tell him about the attack.

And their child.

She shivered.

"Are you cold? I could run back and get your pants or the blanket."

"No, it was just something I was thinking about."

"*Cher*, if your thoughts are so chilling, then let's talk about it."

He used the term of endearment so freely, but it was part of who he was. He'd grown up on the bayous of Louisiana and learned the courtesy of his culture. No matter what kind of training he had, the one from his *grandmère* counted the most. He would always be courteous to women and look out for them. She'd run before he could help her. With his bright future as a Navy SEAL, she wouldn't allow her presence and mistakes to mark his career with a dark blot. She hadn't discovered she was pregnant until weeks later—when she was alone and shattered.

She turned and looked at him straight on. "You've probably guessed some of it—maybe even most of it."

"*Cher*—I," he started, one hand raised.

Charlie shook the gesture off. It was now or never, and never left town sometime back. "Something terrible did happen, Jackson. I've spent the last three years trying to cover it up or erase it, but I can't do it any longer."

"What, *cher*?" he pressed. "What happened?"

"I was raped."

****

Jackson swore prolifically. Creatively.

Falling back on his cultural roots, he bit out a few of the more-explicit Cajun epithets. "The keys are in the jeep. I'll find my own way back."

He spoke through clenched teeth and was even more angry when she looked at him with fear. He looked around for something to punch, and finding nothing, sought his one place of refuge—the sea. Sprinting across the beach, he dove in, cutting through the water with strokes meant to punish. Short of exhausting himself, he was too dangerous to be near anyone. If he'd been off the island, he'd pick a fight with one of the bullies at a local pub. They were tough, but he was tougher. He wouldn't hurt the man, but he'd let off a bit of steam.

His mind grappled with the idea of her being raped, but he couldn't quite grasp it. Why had she run from him? Did she think he'd shun her—look at her with disgust? His gut clenched, and he fought nausea. He made it to one of the coves before he ran from the water and puked. When he could retch no more, he began to sob. His chest and throat tightened while he cried. For their lost love, her pain and suffering, and the difficulties they still had to overcome. He lay in the sand heaving deep breaths when he heard a jeep approaching. Had she followed him? No, this place was off track. Someone who knew him well was looking for him. He didn't want anyone to see him like this, but he was incapable of moving. Drained by the long swim and his emotional outburst, he was toast. All he could do was lie there.

The jeep stopped, and the engine turned off. The bright gleam of a searchlight nearly blinded him.

"I thought you might swim this way." Brandon's voice was neutral. No questions, no lectures about the safety of swimming alone at night.

Jackson opened his eyes when Brandon sank to the sand beside him. "Charlie was raped." All his hurt and anger found its way into the words.

"I know."

Jackson sucked in a painful breath as Brandon's words shot through him like arrows. "What do you mean you know? She just told *me*." He tried to sit up and failed. The shock of the words finally gave way to anger.

Brandon squatted on the sand. "Don't bother trying to punch me. You look done in."

Jackson was sucker punched, but his brain started to kick in. "When did she tell you?"

"The day after it happened, three years ago."

"Why the hell did she tell you, then run from me?" He'd always trusted his friend—had believed him incapable of duplicity. Why had Brandon kept this from him all this time?

"Before you get all bent out of shape, think of what's important here. Charlie came to me after the attack, beaten and hysterical. She refused to call the police—and don't think I didn't try to dissuade her. I did. She said she couldn't face you and wanted to go away. I nursed her for two days, then gave her money and a promise that I was only a phone call away."

Brandon shifted on the sand and plucked at the tiny piece of sea grass by his foot. "She left the next day. I didn't know how she left or where she went. I thought she'd only be gone for a few weeks and then return."

"She said she'd gotten counseling. Why wouldn't she stay and get help? What about a doctor?" Jackson grasped for words. He had so many questions. Charlene must have had her reasons. He'd thought they were perfect together. Maybe she didn't see it the same way. "I still don't understand why *you* didn't tell me. I went out of my mind with worry that she'd been kidnapped or was dead. Couldn't you have at least let me know she was all right?"

"She wasn't all right, and she made me promise to tell no one. You, of all people, should know I keep my promises. Besides, if you had known you would have flown off the handle, left your job, and searched for her. If you want more answers, you'll get them from her. I'd advise you to take it slow. I think seeing you has brought it all back."

Jackson breathed in, clearing his lungs of the tightness seizing them. He'd never felt this much pain. He wasn't angry with Charlie. He was angry about what had been done to her.

"I'm not leaving you here in your condition. Get in the jeep and come to the house."

"No—I'll go to the camp." He couldn't chance meeting her right now. He might do or say something to hurt her even more.

Brandon gave his shoulder a gentle tap. "Will you be okay while I'm gone? I can't put off the mission, and I know a lot has just been dumped on your shoulders. I could leave Rafa in charge."

Anger flared. "I can handle it. I don't want you to worry while you're gone. I'll deal with this and take care of things here."

Brandon stuck out his hand. "Glad to hear it."

Jackson hesitated, then clasped his friend's arm at the elbow. When Brandon returned the clasp, the vow was complete. They were good.

****

Charlene's body shook as she sat on the edge of the chair by her small desk. The menacing look on Jackson's face had frightened her. In the past he'd only given her his flirtatious Cajun look or the heated one—the one where she could feel her bones melting. What she'd glimpsed in his eyes, totally wiped away the Jackson she knew. In his place, a stone-cold killer stared back at her. Was this what he had become since she left? Or had the other Jackson always been there, unseen because of the rosy picture she had painted.

A light tap at her door dragged her back from her reverie. Clasping her shaking hands together, she opened the door. Her hostess stood outside the door. "Mira, you shouldn't be climbing stairs with a tray." She took the tray from the other woman and placed it on the desk.

"I am perfectly capable of handling a few stairs. Now, sit and eat something. This is Dr. Falcon speaking as well as your friend." Mira moved to the end of the bed and sat on the cushioned storage seat. "I've never seen Brandon look so afraid as when you raced into the courtyard honking the horn. Tell me what happened."

Charlene covered her mouth to prevent the sob threatening to undermine what little control she'd gained. She picked up the hot tea and downed half the cup before gasping. She coughed to clear her throat. The damn thing was laced with brandy.

Mira pounded her back. "That should put some color back into your face. Though I suggest you sip the rest."

"Thanks."

She took a bite of the sandwich and nearly threw up. Her emotions were so close to the surface, her stomach felt like it was fighting a storm at sea.

"I know you don't feel like eating but try to keep down a few bites. It'll help you feel strong enough to deal with things. I take it you and Brandon shared a ghastly secret and Jackson didn't know about it."

Charlene swallowed the bite of sandwich, then quickly drowned it with the laced tea. "I like the way you don't sugarcoat things, Mira. I've had it with evasions." She placed the plate on the tray and lifted her chin, ready to speak her truth. "Three years ago, Jackson and I were lovers. I was over the moon in love with him, and I think he felt the same way."

"Go on."

She looked at Mira and took a deep breath. "What has Brandon told you about me?"

"Only that he knew you before, that you're a computer whiz, and you're great at planning. "

Charlene stared in surprise. Brandon Falcon really was a man of his word. She forced another bite down and swallowed the last of the tea. "Three years ago, I became involved in an initiative to have civilians work closely with the military in a special program. We trained like military but acted only as adjunct personnel. Jackson and Brandon were the military trainers in charge of making us civilians into those who could defend themselves if things went south. I excelled at the program and became an expert marksman." She gave Mira a small smile." I've even been known to outshoot that husband of yours."

"I don't believe it. I've seen him hit a target in a rocking boat, wounded, and barely able to hold the gun."

"Said like a good wife. Don't worry, his reputation is safe with me."

Charlene glanced back at the tray and turned the

chair completely away from the desk, continuing her story. "Jackson was in awe of my skills and bought me coffee to learn more about me. We continued with dinner, and three days later, we were in bed. Heat flushed her cheeks, and she looked up to see Mira smiling. "Yeah, I know that it was quick. The program was only six months, and he was set to deploy right afterward."

"Wasn't it against the rules?"

"You betcha. Where I only risked being kicked from the program, Jackson risked his career and a court martial. I would have done anything to prevent that from happening."

"And did you?" Mira asked softly.

"I—"

"Most women would do anything to protect the man they love. I once went into an enemy camp with Rafa to save Brandon." Mira confided.

Charlene caught the faraway look in Mira's eyes. This was another story which needed telling.

Mira started and gave an embarrassed look. "Sorry—lost in the past. What I'm trying to say is, don't be sorry for what you had to do. Decisions made in urgent circumstances aren't always our best, but we have to accept them and live with the consequences."

"Well, tonight, there were consequences to my decisions." Charlene plucked at the edges of her robe, reluctant to broach the painful past. "I was coming home from grocery shopping—it was late, and I was tired. I didn't notice the man hiding behind the hedge until he was on top of me. The harder I fought, the more he hit me. I was nearly unconscious when he raped me."

Mira was off the bench immediately, wrapping her arms around Charlene and gently smoothing the back of her head. Pressed against the physician's abdomen, she felt a hard kick.

"She's offering her comfort, too," Mira murmured.

Charlene sniffled once and then burst into tears. Crying for the pain of losing Jackson, her innocence, and her life. She didn't stop until she was spent. Becoming aware of Mira still standing at her side, she felt guilty and stood. "You should sit." She mopped her face with the cloth napkin on the tray.

"How did you keep the attack from Jackson?"

"I panicked and called Brandon. He insisted I should go to the ER and call the police, but I refused. I was still thinking clear enough to realize an investigation would show whose apartment I'd been in just before I headed to the grocery store and…"

"Jackson would be out of the SEALs." Mira shifted on the seat and rubbed her back. "Charlene, weren't you afraid this man might attack someone else? Your report could have helped."

"If there had been any information, I'd have reported it. He was wearing all black, including a ski mask. He was well-built and muscular—possibly military. That's all I remember. When I came to, he was gone."

"Tell me about today," Mira prompted. "What happened with Jackson? You know as well as I, he would never hurt you. It's only been a week, and I can already see the love in his eyes."

"Things were rough at first, then later during the ride we declared a truce. We completed the tour and went to the beach. I took a nap while he ran. After I woke up, we went for a walk, and I had a flashback. When he asked what frightened me, I just blurted it out. I didn't mean for him to find out like that."

She sent Mira a look which begged for understanding. Swallowing the lump in her throat, she continued. "The change in him was immediate. He handed me the keys and told me to leave. I did, but not before seeing the Jackson I know disappear." She moved to sit beside Mira on the bench. "He became a stranger, Mira. A stranger whose eyes became ice-cold and volcanic-hot at the same time. Afraid of what he might do, I came in with the horn blazing to alert everyone."

Another tap came at the door. Charlene rose and opened it to find Brandon standing outside. She couldn't read anything in his look or stance. "Is he all right?" The question flew from her lips.

He bent to give her a hug, then moved to kiss Mira lightly on the lips. He turned back to her. "He's safe and will be spending the night in the barracks. You only told him part of the story. Wait awhile before dropping the rest on him. I need him emotionally fit enough to trust him with everyone's well-being here on the island."

"But—"

"Talk to me," Mira said. "I'll keep your secret safe. Doctor-patient confidentiality and all that stuff."

"I'll think about it. Thanks for the offer. Now, get yourself off to bed. I'll see you in the morning."

"My sentiments, exactly." Brandon ushered Mira from the room.

After shutting the door, she dressed for bed and slipped under the covers. Sleep—she needed sleep.

Chapter Six

The next morning Charlene crossed the living room quickly and slipped into the office. Boxes still lay in disarray in the small room. She had to come up with a design which encompassed all the new communications equipment, yet still allowed room for the normal desk and filing cabinets. She looked around with streamlining in mind, but there was no way she'd give up the fabulous window view.

As ideas began to flow, she sat and sketched them on paper. Her design would require the services of a carpenter, and that meant she'd have to speak with Jackson. She still hadn't decided what to say to him. They hadn't been alone since their picnic.

The door opened, and without warning the object of her thoughts walked in.

"How's Mira?"

"She's resting. She didn't sleep well, so she drank some special tea to help her sleep. I'll check on her every few minutes to make sure she's okay."

He moved toward Brandon's office without saying more. To keep him there a moment more she asked, "Do we have someone who can do carpentry work? I've drawn up the schematic for the changes needed to accommodate the new equipment. The sooner the structure is in place, the sooner I can get everything up and running." It wasn't what she wanted to say, but maybe talk about them should be kept to a minimum.

"I'll see to it," he said abruptly and closed the door between them.

She took his words for what they were and would not let the tone hurt. To take her mind off things, she pulled a small box off the top of the larger stack. It contained the tracking devices Brandon had ordered. Part of her job was to place one on Mira. They'd argued about whether to tell her, and he'd won. If Mira knew about the device, she might draw attention to it by fiddling with it. Brandon wanted her to be trackable anywhere. After Charlene gave it some thought, she decided a piece of jewelry would be the best bet. To this end, her husband had provided a bracelet.

She slit the box and pulled out the transmitters. Less than a centimeter in length, they could be placed anywhere. The chain bracelet with its single charm would be perfect. Pulling the accounting book from its spot in the bottom drawer, she listed the code for the transmitter in the registry and wrote *Mira's bracelet* across from it. This would allow her to know who or what she was tracking. Having done this, she took out the bracelet, and using a special glue, attached the chip to the oval tag by the clasp. Holding it up to the light, she checked it and saw the chip, only because she knew where to look. Satisfied, she placed the bracelet in her pocket and went to check on Mira.

A quick glance at her watch startled her. She'd been in the office for over two hours. She hastened her steps and pushed gently on Mira's cracked door. Rosita sat in one of the chairs, crocheting a delicate lace dinner mat. A finger to her lips and a nod at the bed let Charlene know Mira was still asleep. She backed out quietly and headed for the veranda. It would be time enough to wake Mira. The lure of the outside was overpowering.

It had been four days since her arrival, and it still felt like she'd been tossed into a whirlwind. The office was tamed but not completely organized. The schematics were complete, as were the specifications to upgrade Mira's security at the lab. She had happily worked her way through the tasks. Now, she faced an unpleasant job. She had to watch as Brandon said goodbye to his wife.

Mira stood, dressed in a green flowing dress. She was the epitome of the beautiful pregnant woman. Charlene squashed a little stab of jealousy and moved to put her arm around Mira's swollen form. Brandon hopped onto the supply boat with his duffel bag in hand. Grief and determination were stamped on his features. Mira didn't cry. She watched the boat until it disappeared from the horizon.

"It's okay to cry, you know," Charlene whispered. "We'll just blame it on the hormones."

Mira shook her head. "I promised him I wouldn't cry, at least while he could see. It tears him apart, and I don't want him distracted. I don't know where he's going or what he's doing, but I know it will be dangerous.

Charlene knew the types of places where these men went and operations they performed, and she worried as much as Mira. Her boss was a good soldier. He'd do whatever he had to and come back home and take up where he'd left off. How did they do it? Separate their job from their lives. Being a good soldier is what gave Jackson that hard edged look that had wiped his youthful exuberance from his face. She urged Mira away from the edge of the dock, needing to get her back to the house before her brave face surely crumpled.

Rafa drove the jeep as close to the dock as possible and opened the door. Jackson placed his palm against Mira's back and led her to the jeep. Once Charlene settled behind Mira, Rafa drove them to the plantation house. Rosita met them at the door and led them through to the master bedroom.

Mira sat on the edge of the bed and picked up the pillow, pressing it to her face.

"Here, *señora*," Rosita urged. "Drink this tea. It will help you rest."

Mira took the cup and slowly drank the chamomile tea. Placing the cup on the side table, she lay back against the pillow.

Charlene closed the blinds and turned out the light. Quietly, she and Rosita left the room.

****

Charlene took a sip of coffee and added another croissant to her plate. She slathered the top with real butter and gleefully watched as it melted and dribbled down the sides. She had to start exercising more if she continued to eat Rosita's baked goods. She watched as Mira followed her example and bit into a heavenly roll. Her eyes were shadowed and a little puffy where she'd finally broken down and cried.

"I'm a terrible influence on you," Mira mumbled around a bite of roll.

"I was just thinking about exercising. Happily, the thought didn't last too long."

Mira laughed and rubbed her rounded belly. "I'm sure I'll get my exercise taking care of this one."

"Are you kidding? With Brandon and the rest of us around, you might need to make an appointment to see your little one."

Voices speaking rapidly in Spanish sounded from the hallway. Rosita came into the kitchen, hesitated, then reached behind her. A small boy, dirty and far too thin, stepped from behind her.

"Doctor, this boy one of the villagers," Rosita said. "He says it's important."

Mira wiped her hands and turned to the boy. " Hello, young man. How can I help you?"

After placing several rolls on a small plate, Charlene motioned the boy to come to the table. He wouldn't sit, but eagerly accepted the food and wolfed down the pastries in two gulps. He cast a wistful eye to the heaped plate on the table but turned his attention back to Mira.

"Please, doctor, *el abuelo* is very sick. My mother says he has fever and goes out of his mind. Can you come?"

Charlene looked at Mira's very-pregnant body and everything protective in her rebelled. She'd only driven through the village and not gone into any of the hovels. Picturing Mira walking through them in her condition sent chills down her spine. Fever meant the man could be contagious.

"Young man, the doctor is very pregnant and should be resting. She—"

"Stop it." Mira interrupted her. "I can't let a man die because my legs are swollen." She turned to Rosita. "Fetch my medical bag, clean sheets, and the new emergency pack that just came in."

"Wait a minute," Charlene protested. "You can't possibly think you're going to the village. You and the baby are my responsibility."

Mira changed like lightning from pregnant woman to doctor-in-charge, in mere seconds. She pushed away from the table and rose with surprising agility. "Then you better get your gun and come with me, because I'm going."

Charlene grabbed the walkie-talkie and clicked the talk button. "Jackson."

Jackson's clipped words came across the device. "What's wrong?"

She suppressed annoyance at his assumption that she was in trouble. "We have a problem. Mira is insisting on going to the village to see an extremely ill patient."

"Dammit, stall her until I get there."

"Got it. Don't dawdle, she's almost ready to leave." She replaced the walkie-talkie and went to help. If left to her own devices, Mira would do everything herself.

Mira paused from sorting her medical supplies. "Are you coming?"

Charlene put an arm around her and gave a squeeze. Technically, she was assigned to be Mira's bodyguard. Admiration for the woman, along with empathy, made her want to be her friend. "Yes. How can I help?"

"You can help me pack these supplies."

Squealing brakes and a racing engine announced Jackson's arrival. He swept into the room, features intent, mouth and fists tight. His eyes seared her with lance-like jabs. "What the hell is going on? It's only my first day as boss, and everyone goes bonkers?"

Mira tensed, and Charlene tightened her arm in reassurance. She recognized his actions. He was angry and worried about his role as leader. The tightened fists were his way of restraining himself. She took in the powerful image he made standing there in his olive-green pants and khaki button-up shirt. Something tightened in her womb.

They were in a tense situation, and she was ogling a man whom she'd given up so many years ago. Why now, when she had this second chance to prove herself? She swallowed, trying to think of something to defuse the tension thickening the air as everyone waited.

The words passed her lips before going through her mind. "Tone it back, Jackson." She knew better than to challenge him. His gaze narrowed on her. Something chilling sparked in his eyes. Her chin lifted, and she met his gaze without flinching.

"Charlie, we'll talk later." He turned his gaze to Mira and his tone softened. "It's all right, *cher*. I'm just anxious about you and the baby. I don't want you to go to the village. You don't know what kind of disease this man might have. He could expose you to something which could hurt you or the baby."

"I'm a doctor. I'm up to date on all my shots. The baby is protected in the womb." She looked around and sat on the arm of the sofa. "I'm going to do my job. I know how to take all the correct precautions."

Charlene watched in awe as the other woman stared the man down.

"I'll drive. Charlie, you take shotgun," Jackson huffed and went outside.

"Well, that was intense, "Mira said.

"He meant well. It's his first day, after all."

She defended Jackson's actions. She didn't blame him. Everyone had to be on guard. Before he left, Brandon had met with them. He'd shown them a report from the coast guard. A band of drug runners acting as pirates were making the smaller islands away from the mainland targets. Unfortunately, Belize was now the hot spot in the Caribbean for drugs and money laundering.

****

Jackson drove with care as the jeep sped over the rough track to the village.

"Try not to hit *all* the holes. It's not much fun after the first fifty or so." Mira's sharp tongue brought a smile to his lips, and he eased back on the accelerator.

"Anything for you, *cher*."

As usual, desolation met them as he entered the main part of the village. Poverty showed in the many repairs made after the last storm. Old signs nailed across holes in the houses bespoke of their poverty as much as the ragged clothes. These poor people had descended from escaped slaves. Still enslaved by their poverty, their only wealth was their strong cultural roots and pride.

The young boy, who'd hitched a ride to play guide, pointed to a hut mounted on stilts by a tall coconut tree. "There, *señor*."

Jackson slowed the jeep and stopped in front of the hut. Jumping out, he helped Mira from the jeep. He grabbed her medical bag, took her by the arm, and led her to the ladder leading up to the door. "We'll have to go single file. Charlie, go first, and I'll be behind her."

He steadied Mira on the ladder as Charlene scrambled up before them. The ladder flexed, and he stopped. "Doc, the ladder won't hold both of us." He dropped the medical bag to the ground and stepped off the ladder. "I'll step off and watch you. Be careful."

****

The smell of sickness hit Mira as she took Charlene's extended hand and pulled herself up the last rung of the makeshift ladder. She'd entered many such rooms—all rife with the smell of unwashed bodies, urine, and the sharp tang of burning incense. In her time spent with Doctors Without Borders, she'd seen worse. At least the roof was sound, and the patient wasn't laying on the muddy ground.

She swallowed hard and focused on the patient. He lay on a pallet on the floor covered with a worn spread. "How long has he been like this?" she asked the woman sitting on a stool by a small table.

"Two days," she said, then identified herself as Marican, the old man's daughter. "The fever keeps going up."

After donning a mask and gloves, Mira bent beside the old man. "Have you given him anything I should know about?"

"I gave him teas made from papaya and guava leaves. For fever, I added boneset."

Most poor countries used folk medicine to treat their patients. If the herbalist or bush medicine woman was knowledgeable, most common ailments could be helped without a doctor. Some remedies were dangerous if not administered correctly. Marican spoke as someone with some knowledge.

Mira gave her a warm smile. "You've done well, Marican, but I think this case might need something more. She inserted the thermometer into his outer ear canal and suppressed a hiss—105 degrees. Not good, especially since he'd received the best homeopathic treatments available. Gently, she pulled the spread from his body. A red rash spread over his sweat-covered chest. His body showed signs of malnutrition.

Jackson touched her shoulder. "Doc, if that rash is contagious, maybe you should let me touch him and you just observe."

"Thank you for the offer but a doctor needs to touch

a patient," she said. "There's something about feeling a person's life force that you can't get by observation. He's not contagious. He has dengue fever. It's transmitted by a mosquito's bite." As she said the words, blood began to trickle from the old man's eyes.

Charlene helped pull her up from the floor. "That can't be good."

Mira turned to Jackson. "He's at the hemorrhagic stage. With his high temperature and the bleeding, he'll die without special treatment."

Jackson shook his head. "Do what you can for him here. We can't leave the island."

"We can't just let him lie here and die," Mira pleaded. "There's a special clinic in Punta Gorda, I worked with the doctor who's in charge of it. It's a short flight. We can have him there in less than two hours."

Charlene moved to stand between the warring factors. "You can't fly at this stage of your pregnancy. The pressure changes could cause you to go into labor."

Mira swallowed the plea she'd been about to present to Jackson. How did Charlene know so much about pregnancy and its idiosyncrasies? She turned away from the three people watching her. She was torn between her need to be a good doctor and her desire to care for her baby. *Brandon, why couldn't you be here to help?* She rubbed her temples where a throb threatened to intensify. Abruptly, she turned back and faced Jackson and Charlene. "You're right. I can't fly or leave the island."

Tension eased the lines of Jackson's face. "I'm glad you see reason."

"You and Charlene can go. Rafa can handle things while Rosita looks out for me."

"You're not serious.

"Oh yes, I am. I can't in good conscience let a man die if there's an alternative. This man may be old, but he's the mainstay of this family. There must be a way to do this."

She watched the play of emotions flit across Jackson's face. His soul was easygoing and his heart as soft as her own. The role of leadership was a hard one for him. She'd seen him with Brandon when they rescued her. He'd done a great job, but he was following Brandon's lead. She hoped this didn't change the happy Cajun's outlook on life. She liked him without the hard edges.

"Doc, you know I can't let you down, and I don't want anyone to die either. Let's get back to the house and figure this out."

Chapter Seven

Charlene watched as Jackson lost the battle with Mira and gave in to her pleas. "All right, Doc. I'll fly him to the clinic. I hope we won't be delivering a corpse."

Mira puffed up and reddened with the effort. "You can't say things like that."

A look of regret flashed over Jackson's face. "I'll do everything I can to get him there alive and safe. Charlie, arrange things with Mira. Pack up the supplies she recommends while Rafa and I work out the management problem."

Rafa came through the door and, with a nod toward Jackson, headed for the conference room. Within an hour, the plane was fueled up and the patient strapped onto the pull-out bed. With luck they'd be there by dark and return the next morning. Punta Gorda was located close to the borders of Belize and Guatemala. Though Guatemala was considered 'safe', certain factions in the political arena tended to stir things up when the mood struck.

Mira was still giving cautions on what to watch for when Jackson nodded to Rafa to close the door. Charlene could only shake her head at his rudeness as he completed the precheck and gently pushed the throttle. The plane lifted off the water and gained altitude. After banking, he turned south toward Punta Gorda.

Charlene tucked the sheet around the old man and

strapped him in. Jackson's remark had been crass and totally unnecessary. He could be right, though. The old man was barely hanging on. His breathing was labored, and blood began to trickle from his nose. He was at a critical stage. "How long does the trip take?"

Jackson looked back at her and pointed to the earphones. He hadn't heard her. She unstrapped from the pull-down seat and headed for the copilot's seat. Strapping in, she put the headphones on her head and repeated her question. "How long will the trip take?"

Jackson turned back to the front window. "With no problems, it should take about three hours. It'll be dark when we arrive. The port where I need to land is shady. We'll have to take special care."

Charlene thought about what he'd said, then nodded. "I need to keep checking him, so I'll sit in the back."

"Put on those gloves Doc gave you. It's best not to take chances."

Charlene checked on the old man and wiped the blood oozing from his mouth. The only sick person she'd taken care of was her daughter. As if her thoughts could be heard by the man flying the plane, her hand jerked. How would he react if he knew? She closed her eyes trying to blot out the image of the rage on Jackson's face. She had cheated him of two years of his daughter's life.

The old man coughed, and she turned his head to keep him from drowning in his own blood. His face was hot, and she took out a bottle of water and dampened the cloth. Gently, she patted his face and neck with the cool water. His skin burned her fingers through the cloth. She dribbled some of the water into his mouth, catching the excess that ran out.

The plane jerked then dropped altitude quickly.

Charlene fell backward to the floor.

Jackson craned his neck to check on her. "Charlie! Are you okay?"

Stunned by the fall, it took several moments for the throbbing in her head to kick in.

He slid one side of the earphones off his ear and swung around toward her. "Charlene?"

"I'm okay. Just stunned."

"Don't try to stand. Crawl up here and strap in. This weather came out of nowhere."

"What about our patient?"

She rolled over, fighting dizziness as the plane continued to dip and sway. Her progress was slow as she moved along the floor. She reached the front and crawled into the seat. With shaking fingers, she buckled in. A warm hand touched her arm, bringing comfort. The brief touch ended as Jackson slipped the earphone back in place and began a conversation with some air traffic controller.

"How large is it?" He used a marker to jot numbers on a dry erase board. "How far to go around?" He jotted more numbers. "We have a critically ill patient with dengue fever aboard. We are heading to the Punta Gorda research clinic."

Charlene listened to his calm voice and admired his ability to function under duress. His SEAL training had honed his natural easygoing nature into someone who could handle emergency situations with ease. He'd grown up so much since their relationship ended. He'd become a man—a man she was dangerously attracted to.

He'll never forgive you.

Wind buffeted the small plane, causing it to bounce up and down. Jackson switched the dial, and a click came over her headphones.

"This is some freak storm. It wasn't on the radar when I checked before we took off. Punta Gorda air control has directed me to go around it."

"How long will it take? El grandfather doesn't have time to waste." Charlene glanced back at the poor man strapped to the bed. Blood continued to ooze from his mouth, and she unclipped her buckle.

"No, it isn't safe. There's no telling which way the wind will bump us. You could end up hitting your head on something. Stay put."

Faced with the dilemma of something happening to the patient and her getting hurt tore at her. She'd be willing to risk it, but something in Jackson's voice gave her pause. Turning to face him, she noticed the strain around his eyes and mouth. He wasn't telling her everything. "What is it?"

"We aren't landing at the airport. We're landing at the harbor. The clinic is only a block from there. There's more." He stopped talking as the plane dipped once more.

Charlene grabbed the edge of the seat and held on. Her stomach pitched with the plane, and she swallowed hard to keep her stomach contents from ending up on the windshield. When the plane leveled out, she turned back to face him. "What are you trying to tell me?"

Jackson flipped another switch then turned to her. "Today is election day. Crowds will come in to the town from the surrounding villages to vote. This election is quite volatile. Besides, locals use it as an excuse to get crazy drunk. Things could get dicey."

"I've got my gun and an extra clip."

Jackson flashed her a smile. "I knew I could count

on you to be prepared. This storm could get violent, just like the elections."

"How long to go around? She knew she wasn't going to like his answer before the words left his lips. He always chewed the side of his mouth when things were tough. Not that she'd ever mention it to him. More than once she'd won a poker hand with such knowledge.

"It'll take at least an extra hour and half. Do you think he has that long?"

He was asking her? Like she had any special medical knowledge. "I don't know, but I'd say any extra time would make his chances slimmer."

He nodded and turned a dial on the dash. "*Punta Gorda, be advised private plane Darlin #270483JF will continue current course. This is a medical emergency.*" He listened to the person on the other end, then turned the dial off. "Well, the die have been cast."

Charlene swallowed hard and faced the front windshield. Water droplets began to form tiny rivers, running to the sides. The wipers swiped the glass but made little difference. She wanted to say something—ask questions, but she was afraid. He'd made a hard decision, risking both their lives for their patient. She'd have done the same.

Lightning flashed, creating an x-ray glow against the swiftly moving clouds. Charlene swallowed hard. She supposed it was too late to tell Jackson she was a little scared of flying. Wind buffeted the plane, sending it first one way and then the other. Jackson's face took on a grim look as he gripped the steering wheel with crushing force. An hour passed and the skies cleared a little. The darkness before them began to lighten as they got closer to their destination, and by the time they were over Punta Gorda, the last rays of a beautiful sunset shot spears of light across the plane.

****

Jackson took it all in. He never got tired of it. Flying into a world of color. A quick flyover showed the port was very busy. Jackson would have to tie up at the far end. Not the best place to leave his beloved plane. Charlene glanced at him. When he pointedly looked at her clenched hands, she relaxed them.

"You must have been terrified," he said.

"I was scared, but I knew you wouldn't let anything happen to us."

"Thanks for the faith, *cher*, but sometimes it's out of my hands."

"You wouldn't do anything if it wasn't done well. If that's faith, then so be it."

"We'll be landing soon, then coast into the harbor proper. It might mean a hike. Are you ready?"

Charlene smiled at him. "Yes, Captain. I'm ready."

Chapter Eight

After Jackson banked the plane, he circled back toward the port. Like the lady she was, *Darlin* gently touched down on the azure-blue water. Views of boats, trees, and buildings flew past as he pushed the throttle and slowed the plane. Coming to a halt, he turned the plane around and coasted to the far end of the dock.

"That was fun." Charlene laughed. "Let's hope the delivery of our patient is as easy." She unbuckled and ran to the old man while the plane drifted the last few yards.

"How is he?"

"Not good. His coloring is too white. He's probably bleeding internally."

"Well, as soon as I secure the plane, we'll be off." He looked with disgust at the trash floating in the harbor. People here knew the dangers of pollution. Much of their livelihood depended upon tourism. This unsightly mess wouldn't draw many crowds. Not to mention the harm to the reef.

Thirty minutes later, he and Charlene were hoofing down the dock, their patient on a stretcher between them. Jackson didn't like the idea of being in a position where his hands weren't free. Especially with the present crowd. Mostly drunk and excited, the men and women they passed ignored them. Intent on their fun, two Americanos with a stretcher were hardly exciting enough to cause them to notice.

The door to the clinic was locked—a testament to the high crime and fear of drug traffickers. Any clinic where pain medication was administered had to guard against raiders looking to score. This clinic even had barred the windows, making it appear closed. They climbed the steps and gently lowered the stretcher to the porch floor.

"You look meaner than me; you knock," Charlene murmured.

He laughed. Even amid possible danger, Charlie could make him laugh. "Okay, I'll be the ogre." He raised his hand and knocked on the wooden door. When no one answered, he pounded his fist against the panel.

A three-by-five inset opened, and a pair of steely black eyes looked back at him. "Go away. You will get nothing here."

When the tiny opening tried to close, Jackson struck the space with his fist and made hard contact with a face. "We have an emergency patient from Dr. Mira Falcon. We are expected."

Voices argued in Spanish as he rubbed the back of his knuckles against his trousers. He hadn't meant to break the man's nose, but this was an emergency. The talk ended, and the sound of several locks opening drew his gaze to the doorknob. Two men came out, one flitting a nervous gaze around the street, the other holding a bleeding nose.

"Quickly, get in before anyone sees."

Jackson pointed to the stretcher and the two men carried the patient inside. Charlene followed the man with the bleeding nose.

Nose man began locking the four locks affixed to the door.

"The last room on the left. John, hurry and open the door. My name is Marco Castillo, by the way. I was glad to hear from my old friend. We worked together in Doctors Without Borders."

"Good to meet you, Doctor. We had a bumpy ride getting him here," Jackson said as he placed his end of the stretcher on the edge of the hospital bed. A nurse in a starched white uniform entered the room, and the four of them settled the patient on the bed.

Dr. Castillo turned to the nurse. "Set up an IV and draw blood. We need to cross and match for a transfusion."

Charlene stepped forward. "I hope he'll be okay. His grandson loves him so much."

"Well, young lady, I've seen love cure a lot of things. It never hurts to have loved ones rooting for you. At a quick glance, this man has a fifty-fifty chance of surviving the night. That love you talk about could tip the balance."

Jackson touched her arm to motion her out of the room. He could tell she'd already formed an attachment to the boy and his grandfather and hoped she wouldn't get her heart broken. He knew the pain. Thinking her dead for the past three years nearly killed him. Finding out why she left hurt as much if not more. His mind shied from those thoughts. If he could block it, he could deal with it. His responsibility to the team and its members was greater than his need for retribution or resolution. *Like hell it was.*

He drew her into the hallway. "Let's try to find a quiet spot for some food. I'm leery of the hotels. We might have to sleep on the plane. You good with that?"

She stared at him as if searching for something

behind his words. Finally, her face brightened. "Let's find a place that serves alcohol. I could use a stiff drink after that storm."

"Be honest. It was the plane ride which scared you the most."

The door to the room opened, and Dr. Castillo came out. "I'm sorry you've had such a poor welcome. The patient is in bad shape and must have treatment immediately. Will you give my regards to Mira, please?" With those words, the man disappeared back into the room.

"Let's get out of here." He took her arm and headed to the door. John was there to assist with the locks, and Jackson heard them slide into place as soon as the door closed.

After the saner environment of the clinic, the sounds of glass breaking, people shouting, and endless numbers of bodies pushing and shoving against one another put a damper on Jackson's upbeat mood. He'd thought they could check into a nice hotel, have dinner, and talk. The talk they should have had but he'd opted to run away in anger. God, he must have frightened her. Would he ever be able to convince her he'd had her best interests at heart?

Charlene stumbled as a drunken couple lost their balance and fell into her. With snake-like reflexes, Jackson caught her and pulled her close beside him. Tightening his arm around her back, he searched for a less-crowded spot so he could plan.

"There's no way we'll find a sit-down place for dinner. Let's look for some local fast food and we'll take it back to the plane."

"I think we should follow that fantastic smell."

Across the street, delicious aromas came from a tiny business on wheels that was positioned between two adobe buildings. Smoke rose from the cart, and cheerful laughter rose from the people near it. He glanced at the sea of people between them and the food and sighed. He tightened his hold on Charlene and waded in.

The first yard was smooth going. People parted and let them pass. As they reached the center of the crowd, things got tense. People pushed and shoved. The overpowering pressure of bodies smashed against them, and he feared they'd be trampled. He struck out, elbowing a giant of a man. Before the man could retaliate, the crowd pushed him farther down the street.

"Hurry." Charlene tugged his other arm. "There's an opening."

Jackson let her lead them to a thinning section of the crowd. Another minute, and they were standing in front of the cart. If heaven had a smell, this was it. His gaze roamed the pictures. "Four panadas, a dozen tamales, and two cervezas, *por favor*." Languages weren't his forte, but any guy could order fast food and beer in almost any country.

"*Si, señor*."

He handed the man a large bill and shook his head when the vendor started to make change. The man's eyes lit up, and a smile broadened his face. He wrapped the meat pies in paper and placed the tamales in a paper carton. Reaching behind the cart, he pulled the beers from a cooler. Unexpectedly, he pulled up a second cooler and indicated they should sit.

"I think we've been given the best seat in the house." He followed Charlene around the cart and sat across from her on the cooler "Sorry about the beer, but it's the safest thing to drink."

"This is fine. I don't think I could have made it all the way back without food. Weren't you being a little 'big eyed'? I'll probably only eat two tamales and a meat pie."

"I was counting on it. I'm famished." He laughed at her incredulous face. "I'm a big eater, remember?" He nearly bit his tongue when her face instantly changed. She obviously remembered a lot of things. He stuffed a tamale in his mouth to keep it shut. Now was not the time for conversation.

"This is nice—being away from the crowd like this. How long should it take to get back to the plane?"

Jackson considered her question. Was she ready to be to be in the tight confines of the plane alone with him all night? He hadn't thought that far ahead. Of course, it was an excellent place for them to talk. The crowd noise faded as she bit into the meat pie and made the cutest noise in her throat. Damn, he was a goner, sitting here watching her eat food while his uncontrolled libido did a liftoff. He swallowed hard and shifted on the cooler, trying to gain some comfort.

She finished the bite and her eyes popped open. "These are fantastic. We'll have to get Ana and Rosita to cook these."

"You still enjoy the simple things, don't you?"

Charlene paused and then tilted her head. "Don't you?"

Uncomfortable with her inquisitive stare, he sat back and studied the crowd around the edge of the cart. They were protected by the cart, but he needed to keep an eye on the crowd. Alcohol and zealots didn't mix well. Most of the men would carry some sort of weapon.

Sooner rather than later, someone would get hurt here tonight.

A loud roar rose in the street to their left. Shouts and curses followed by glass breaking had him on his feet. A large stone struck the cart as others rained down on the adobe buildings. “It’s starting to get dangerous. Stay close to me no matter what.”

Charlene gripped his arm with one hand and held the bag of food tightly in the other. “My mama didn’t raise no fool.”

He tried to stick to the sidewalk as people ran and bottles and bricks smashed into windows. A woman fell beside him, the ugly crowd nearly trampling her before he pulled her out of the way. He weaved in and out of the maze of bodies, keeping the harbor lights in sight. The crowd began to thin as they moved away from the main area. The smell of the ocean wafted up, cleansing after the stench of booze and bodies.

After dodging the last of the rioters and flying bottles, Jackson and Charlene reached the dock where they had tethered the plane. A knot began to form in his stomach as the people around them became seedier. Here were the pickpockets, hustlers, and prostitutes. Those, he could handle. It was those he didn’t see causing his hackles to rise. The harbor wasn’t in the safest part of town, and the dock they’d been forced to use was very dark and out in the open.

He slowed his steps, pushing Charlene behind him. He felt her pull her gun at the same time he did. *Good girl*. It made him proud that his Charlie could defend herself. Unless she was physically overwhelmed, she’d take out any threat.

He stopped, a finger to his lips to warn her, then he

stepped with her into the shadow of a low hanging vine on the wall. His bad guy radar was pinging big time. When his hand began to itch, he became alarmed. His New Orleans *mojo* had never let him down. When the itching started, the bullets would soon follow.

Flak from the wall exploded at his face. He covered his face and dropped to the ground. The shot had come from one of the boats tied to the dock. He'd give anything for his night-vision goggles.

"Cover me," he whispered in her ear. "I'm going to check the boats."

She didn't protest, just nodded. He moved out of the shadows and ran toward the wooden dock. Dropping behind a trash can, he surveyed the boats lined up near him. They all looked deserted, but he knew better. Someone was out there shooting at him with a silenced gun. Not some mugger—someone higher on the food chain. His guess was a drug smuggler. After his plane most likely.

Two shots rang out and Charlene ran, then rolled toward him. He grabbed her arm and pushed her against the solid can. "What the hell, Charlie? I thought it was understood you'd stay put."

"Yeah, and how would I see you when you got on the boats? I saw movement two boats down. There were two of them. I think I winged one."

She said it so matter of fact it made him smile. There was a note of excitement in her voice. He was all for confidence, but Lord save him from overzealous backup. "This trash can is your friend. You hear me? I'm going to move down to the boat. Don't follow, and don't shoot me by mistake."

The last was an insult. She never missed the target,

but this was different from shooting a paper target. This was real life and death. He took a deep breath and released it. Rolling to his feet, he skulked behind the only cover he had, the pier piles. Not much cover, but with the shadow cast by the moon, the support poles could save his life.

A bullet hit the decking beside him. He was too exposed. He set his gun down and removed his shoes. Time to do what he was trained to do. Without a sound, he slipped into the warm water. Sliding under the dock, he swam silently toward the boat where the shot had come from. He heard movement near the bow and sank below the surface. He found the anchor rope and climbed up slowly.

The boat dipped and he froze. The bastard was heading for Charlene. She fired a shot and the man dropped. With a strong kick, he was at the dock within seconds. Using the pile support he climbed up. Charlene walked toward him, arms straight in front of her, gun steady. The man didn't move.

She kept the gun aimed at the man lying prone on the decking. "He's wounded but not dead."

"You're handy to have around." Jackson checked the man and found his left arm bleeding, but he was alive. He grabbed his gun and put on his shoes. He returned and removed the man's shirt, tearing it into strips to bind his hands. "Let's get out of here before someone comes. We can't risk being questioned by the police."

"All right by me. He won't die, will he? I've never killed anyone."

"No, someone will wander this way and find him soon." He turned and hurried to where he'd left the plane.

Only it wasn't there. Adrenaline rushed through his body as he searched the water. There—the plane was adrift, and someone was trying to get on board.

"Wait here. I'll take care of the scumbag who's messing with *Darlin.* Once I get it started, I'll come back and pick you up."

"But—"

Her words cut off as he ignored the trash and debris and dove into the murky water. With powerful strokes he swam toward the plane. The man trying to get aboard banged at the door with something metal. Jackson cringed, thinking of the cost of paint and repairs. He'd make the idiot pay.

A small explosion lit up the plane, highlighting the would-be plane jacker. He smiled. That booby trap worked every time. He always rigged the door when he left the plane in questionable moorings. The trap was mostly sound and light with a little smoke thrown in for show. It usually frightened the perp away. It would only take a few minutes to fix. The guy was stunned, but still clung to the plane.

Reaching up, he grabbed the man's foot and pulled him into the water—his domain. Though the man threw a few punches, he had little fight in him. Jackson punched his face, allowing him to fall on his back. With a shove, he pushed the unconscious man away. His *mojo* kicked in and he turned swiftly, ready to punch.

"Wait, it's me," Charlene yelped and plunged backward.

"What the hell are you doing? I told you to wait." Fear for her made his words sharp. Dammit, he could have hit her.

"There were people coming. I had to get out."

"All right, hang on to the side while I fix the mess left by that jackass."

"You're in a foul humor."

"I wasn't finished with the tamales, and he scratched *Darlin's* paint."

Charlene laughed then swam the few feet to the grab bar on the plane. "Whew, I'd hate to be the one to come between you two."

"Just keep that in mind, *cher*." he said vaguely.

What he really wanted to say was he never wanted anything to come between them. The thought gave his heart a jolt. *Slow down*—his sanity tried to kick in. There was a whole lot of water under that bridge. He took out his knife and cleared the wiring off the door lock. The quiet alerted him; he turned to her. "You okay, Charlie?"

"Yeah, just thinking."

He flipped open the inset and keyed in the code. "Well, think quick because it's time to go." He put his hand down and pulled her onto the ladder and helped her into the plane. With haste, he buckled in and hurried the pre-flight checklist. He didn't want to fly at night, but they had to leave Punta Gorda now. An official investigation would keep him away from the plantation. Mira needed him and Charlene to keep her safe.

The engines started, and the propellers sprang into full spin. He pulled back on the throttle, and the plane pushed forward. A red light flashed on the instrument panel. Shit—they hadn't refueled. He kept the news to himself and turned off the flasher. The light remained, but it didn't look so alarming. "We're only going a few miles. It's too dangerous flying at night."

"Um, what's the red light?"

"We just need a little gas, that's all."

Her voice rose above the noise of the plane as he took off. “That’s all?”

He flew low and east. There were several cayes a few miles out. They’d wait until morning and then worry about how to get home.

Chapter Nine

"I don't want to risk flying the plane in the dark without a complete inspection. We're going to set down by one of the small islets. They're isolated enough to keep us out of harm's way."

"You're just going to park this thing on the water by an island in the dark? Isn't that a little dangerous?"

"*Cher*, have a little faith. I could fly this thing with my eyes closed."

"Don't you dare. Keep them focused forward, please."

He dipped the plane just a little to get a reaction from her. It came quickly. She jabbed him in the arm, hard. She also smiled. Something eased in the pit of his stomach. They were good.

He set the heading on the dash and concentrated on the window in front of him. The atmosphere eased, and things became comfortable once more. Twenty minutes later, a dark shape showed on the horizon. Moonlight shone on the beaches of the small islet. He wasn't sure of the name for this one, but waves broke on the reef far enough from shore to let him land.

"It's so beautiful from up here. The sand almost sparkles in the moonlight."

"It's phosphorescent plankton. Certain times during the year, it covers the sand and water, making for a magical sight. Of course, you have to be in the sky to appreciate the whole effect." He dropped in altitude and slowed their air speed. *Darlin* touched down as light as a dragonfly on a pond.

Charlene unlatched her belt and turned to face him. "You never expressed an interest in flying while we were together."

"*Cher*, I didn't think about a lot of things back then. Seems my mind and body were otherwise occupied."

"Yes, well, um…"

"Don't tell me you're embarrassed by what we shared." He cut the engine as he felt the tug of sand on the bottom of the plane. "I rather thought you enjoyed it as much as I did."

"I don't think now is the time to discuss it."

"*It*? So, our relationship has been downgraded to an abstract pronoun?"

Unfastening his belt, he slipped off his shoes, and opened the door. "I need to tether the plane. You could take a walk on the beach if you like."

He dropped from the plane, landing in waist-high water. Sloshing forward, he removed the anchor from its security hook and waded ashore. She watched him become a shadow on the sand, then shut the door. She didn't feel like getting wet just now. What they'd been through on the streets left her feeling tense. The crease in her forehead and an ache behind her eyes came courtesy of Jackson. Though he'd protected her in the streets, then flown them to safety, he'd allowed his foul humor to spill over onto her. How she could be so irritated and yet so attracted to a man at the same time defied logic.

The plane dipped as Jackson reclimbed the ladder. His gaze caught hers as he entered.

She watched him finish rechecking the plane before he closed the door for the night. "We need to talk."

She'd expected the words, yet they still jarred. They would be alone on the plane all night. What would she say to him? How did she start? "Where are your medicated wipes?"

"Did you step on something? Let me see." He was on his knees before she could stop him.

She looked down and couldn't resist the look of concern on his face. Cupping his cheek with her palm, she ran her thumb gently over his lips. At the touch, her womb clinched. She squelched the inner voice telling her to dip down and capture those lips. Now was not the time. "I'm fine. I thought I'd take the opportunity to sanitize the bed where our patient slept."

He stiffened, then stood. "Good idea."

He pulled open a cupboard door and extracted the needed materials. Handing them to her, he moved to the cot and stripped the bedding before she could touch it. He handed her some gloves and moved to the back of the plane.

She began wiping the railings and plastic-covered mattress. The reason for the covering gave her pause. How many wounded men had lain on this bunk? "Jackson? I wasn't trying to put you off. I need to keep busy, is all. Ask me what you want to know."

He stalked to her and stopped mere inches from where she stood. "Why didn't you trust me? I loved you more than life itself. I'd have done anything for you. Why didn't you let me help you through it?"

His words were bitter, torn from his pain-filled heart. They hit her like bullets, wounded like barbs. How could she deny he was right? They'd been in a close relationship, shared everything, and then she'd run away. "I know how much I hurt you, and I'm sorry."

"Sorry? Hell, you ripped my life apart, and that's all you can say? I thought you were dead for three years. If you didn't want to be with me, you could have at least let me know you were alive. Was that too much to ask?"

She refused to allow the tears that burned behind her lids to fall. She knew they would stop all conversation. This had to be worked out. "If I'd let you know, you would have gone crazy looking for the man who hurt me." Her words burst out.

"You're damn right I would. A man has a right to protect the woman he loves."

"At what cost? Your career? Your freedom. I know you—or thought I did. You would have felt honor bound to avenge me. You'd have probably killed the man responsible and ended up in prison. I didn't want that for you."

"If I'd found him, you can bet he wouldn't be walking around today." He paced back and forth in the minuscule confines of the plane. "I'm a trained killer, *cher*. No one would have found the body."

She gasped and threw the wipes in the trash. "How can you say such things? The man I knew wasn't capable of murder."

"I'm not the boy you once knew. I grew up after you ripped my heart out by leaving. I'm capable of revenge, and my conscience would be clear."

She took another wipe and cleaned her hands. This was going so badly. Moving to the side of the plane, she pulled down a jump seat. She regretted sitting immediately. He continued to stand, towering over her. "You're forgetting something."

He whipped around to stare at her face. "What?"

She swallowed hard and took a deep breath. "My emotional state. I was shattered—scared. One thing did stay in the front of my mind. If I'd reported the attack, there would have been an investigation which would have exposed our relationship and ended both our careers. You were my superior and my instructor. If they knew you were sleeping with me, it would have been over for you. I couldn't let that happen. If my life was in ruins, I wanted yours to be safe."

She jerked out of her seat and moved to the back of the plane. The small door to the restroom was ajar, and she took refuge, closing and locking the door behind her.

"Do you think running away from me again is the answer, *cher*?"

His voice just outside the door nearly melted her bones. His Cajun accent had thickened, letting her know the depth of his feelings. "I don't have all the answers, Jackson. I did what I thought I had to do. I can't undo the past."

"You can talk about it. Help me to understand."

Charlene looked everywhere but at the man who meant everything to her. She unlocked the door and came up short as he stood in the doorway. "Why can't you leave it in the past?"

He ran a gentle finger across her cheek. "Because I care. We were split apart by circumstances once before. Why can't we grab the second chance we've been given and run with it?"

Guilt squeezed her heart. Why couldn't she say the words—tell him the whole truth? "It's complicated. I'm not sure we can ever be together again."

He dropped his hand and stood back, allowing her

to come out of the tiny room. “Why can’t we? What stands in our way?”

The time had come, she had to get the entire truth out into the open. “Sit down, Jackson.” Her words were quiet but acted on him like a sledgehammer. He sat in the chair she had recently occupied. He waited, his eyes watching her face, his body still. It was as if he knew the next words out of her mouth would change their lives forever. “There is a child.” She watched the shock, confusion, and anger register in his face.

He jumped from the seat and took her by the shoulders. “You got pregnant by the man who raped you?”

Anger changed to disgust. His stare ran up and down her body, and his fingers clenched on her upper arms. She ignored the pain, allowed him his feelings. “No, I had our child.”

“What?” He turned his back and reached inside another cabinet. He pulled a beer and a soda from the small refrigerator. “This conversation is too intense for in here. Let’s go for a walk.” He grabbed a blanket and pack, then left the plane without looking back.

It was time for this to end. She had to make it right.

****

The water felt cool after the heated conversation. Rather than walk, she swam the few yards to the shore. He had spread the blanket on the sand next to a lantern which must have been in the pack. He was nowhere in sight. Had he run like she had? Breaking branches drew her attention to the shrubs which grew behind the grasses. Relieved, she turned to the blanket and sat. The breeze chilled her as it blew across her wet clothes. She was tempted to strip out of them but thought better of it.

He dropped the limbs onto the sand. “I’ve got some branches for a fire.”

Her gaze followed his movements as he used his heel to dig a depression in the sand, then laid the branches in a tent-like method. He opened the pack and pulled a cigarette lighter from inside and lit the small amount of wadding he’d added. When the small fire blazed, he placed some dry coconut shells on top and sat back on his haunches.

“I can’t believe you kept knowledge of my child from me all this time.”

She felt the impact of his words and reeled back as if he’d struck her. How could he be so cruel?

“I know that hurts the most, but I couldn’t exactly call you up one day and say—by the way, we made a child together. For months I was afraid the baby *was* his. At three months I went for genetic testing. I was so happy to know it was yours. I did try to contact you then—but you’d been deployed.”

“There are ways to contact us, as you well knew. Why did you ignore them and deny me access to our child?”

“Hope. Her name is Hope.”

His head jerked up and his eyes blazed. Was it anger or anguish? She couldn’t tell.

Chapter Ten

Jackson fought to remain in control. A few days ago, his rage had scared her. His responses in the next few minutes could decide the relationship between them forever. He sucked in a calming breath but couldn't stop the searing pain in his heart. Even wounded and trapped in Afghanistan, the pain hadn't been like this. He felt like his flesh had been filleted. How the hell was he going to keep a civil tongue when all he could think of was lashing out?

"I have a daughter?"

"Yes, she's a little over two years old, healthy, and has your eyes."

Another jab to his heart. "Tell me about her. Where is she?"

Charlene shifted on the blanket and stared at him across the flames. "She's with my aunt in Georgia. When Brandon recruited me for this job, I almost didn't come. I knew I'd hurt you badly, but looking into those eyes so like yours, I knew I had to tell you. You deserve the right to know your child."

"You had no right to keep her from me. I never hurt you or did anything to deserve this."

Clipped and filled with pain, the words tore from his lips. His mind was a whirlwind of thoughts—his heart churned with emotion. Could they overcome this? Did he want to? *Hell, yes.* Nothing would keep him from his daughter now he knew of her existence.

"I had every right to keep her a secret," she retorted. "There were no ties between us—only passion. Plus, the program was only for six months. Afterward, you would have deployed and—"

The sound of the waves lapping the shore seemed louder with her sudden silence. He pulled in a deep breath of the salty smell. The devil on his shoulder had egged him on, going around and around the same thing. His hurt was too fresh—the anger too hot. "I want to be with my child, *cher*. I want to watch her grow, catch up on what I've missed." He stood, suddenly restless. "A lot of things have happened to us in the last three years. Let's find a way to fix it."

Unwilling to say something else to upset things, he stripped and went into the sea. The water had always been a balm to his soul. He let it rinse the smell of anger and pain from his skin. If only he could wash it from his soul as easily.

****

Charlene's hands fisted as he disappeared beneath the surface of the water. Tension mounted when he remained hidden. Her breath released as his head popped up in the distance. Swimming alone at night wasn't safe. Weren't there sharks? Hell, he was a SEAL for God's sake. What was she worried about? Indecision made her antsy, so she stood and removed her clothing—all of it. Words weren't working so she'd give in to her desire. She wanted him with every fiber of her being.

The tide had changed, raising the height of the water close to shore. She stood at the edge, allowing the sand to flow beneath her feet as the water retreated. Gathering her courage, she entered the water, kicking her legs just enough to stay afloat. Turning onto her stomach, she swam toward the reef. She swam with punishing strokes, her body sliding smoothly through the water. It felt like satin as it slid across her skin. Lost in the sensations of the water, she jerked wildly when something bumped her. Thrashing in her panic, she had visions of sharks in her mind when strong arms grabbed her.

"It's me, Charlie. You're okay."

Relief swamped her and she sagged against him. Awareness sparked as her skin met his. Excitement skittered down her spine as his powerful kicks brought his sex up against hers.

"I'm sorry," he breathed out the words. "It's so dammed frustrating."

Without warning, he swooped down and touched his lips to hers. She gave up all pretense of treading water. Instead, she clung to him as he managed to keep them both afloat and still kiss her senseless. He'd always managed to make her toes curl when he kissed her. His lips were hard against hers, then his tongue invaded her mouth—dancing with hers in a duel of mating.

Water covered her chin, and she pulled back, moving her legs to stay afloat. "I don't fancy drowning, tonight—no matter how good your lips taste."

He growled deep in his throat and reached for her again. Before he could touch her, she struck out for the shore. With brisk shakes she flung the water from her hair. The sand crunched as she moved to the blanket. The breeze blew across her skin, tautening her nipples. She felt his gaze burning into her back—knew it roamed slowly.

His fingers touched her from behind. Her skin rippled with sensation and her breasts ached. Before her mind could form the thought, his large hands moved around to cup each mound.

"My God, I've dreamed of this for years. I thought I was crazy, imagining you out there somewhere, waiting for me to come to you."

His voice sent warm air against her ear. He was a master at making her feel every sensation as an invasion of pleasure. How she'd missed this. He was very tactile and used his fingers to trace patterns on her chest before sliding them in a teasing whisper of pleasure across her belly. Her womb tightened—yet still he touched with only his fingers. Magical as they were, she longed for his hands to knead her flesh, to pull her against his body.

"Stop teasing and let me feel you," she said.

"I need to relearn the secrets of your body. We have plenty of time."

His words created images in her mind that should make her blush. Instead, she grew more aroused. When his arms encircled her, she gasped at the overwhelming flash of sensation of his skin against hers. How had she ever lived through this before?

"I think you know too much already." She laughed as his bristled chin rubbed against her neck. His lips followed, causing her to arch her neck, reaching for more.

"It's what you do with knowledge that counts." He continued to ply her neck with nibbles, then used one hand to pull her back hard against his swollen sex.

She cried out and her knees buckled. Landing on the blanket, she clutched at it as he followed her down. He was careful not to land on her. Unable to stand it any longer, she turned and ran her hands across his chest. His steely muscles flexed at her touch, and a sexy male growl erupted from his throat.

"I forgot how bold you can be. Touch me, *cher*. Let your fingers feel my need." His accent thickened.

She loved that about him. He allowed her to explore with abandon and enjoyed her boldness. Her hands roamed familiar territory and paused at a puckered scar below his nipple.

"What happened?" She ran her fingertips lightly around the flesh.

"You know I can't—"

"Stuff the regulations, Jackson. It's just you and me and I need to know."

"It was a knife. I slipped on some street debris and the target temporarily got the upper hand. It's fine now. Don't fret."

In answer, she lowered her lips to the spot and kissed it lightly.

"*Cher*," he hissed. He drew her closer, claiming her lips, and she was lost. When the weight of his body settled over her, she sighed with pleasure. She wrapped her legs around his thighs as he continued to ravage her lips.

"Are you sure, Charlie?"

His whispered question could have pulled her from the moment, instead it pulled at her heartstrings. This big powerful man, someone she'd nearly destroyed, had asked her if she was certain. She didn't know all the answers and could only guess at how difficult it was for him to give her the choice. He may not still love her, but he cared.

"Don't worry; I'm on the pill."

His body tensed at her words.

"That wasn't what you meant, was it?" Pulling back

from him she stared up into his face. He'd become adept at hiding his emotions since they were together. The eyes gave him away. Placing her palm against his cheek, she gazed into his burning stare "I don't know if things can be fixed between us, Jackson, but I'm willing to try. As for being sure—right now, I've never been as sure of anything in my life."

His head swooped down once more, capturing her lips in a hungry assault. She gave kiss for kiss and moaned a deep cry of pleasure as he joined their bodies.

"You're so dammed beautiful. Do you know how sexy you are with your sparkling eyes and a body forged in heaven?"

"Your eyesight and your flattery have improved." He thrust deeply and she cried out. "Don't stop. I love how strong your body is and how gentle your hands are." He used those hands to trace her hips, then touched her nub lightly. Her body tensed with sensation, and she grabbed on to him, pushing back, reaching for bliss. She heard his guttural cry as she fell off the edge and shattered into a million chards. Afterward, he rolled, allowing her to be on top, and just held her. She breathed in his scent, touched the fine hairs on his chest, and felt complete.

Chapter Eleven

Mira leaned forward and grabbed the edge of the planting table. With a sigh, she arched her back, trying to stretch the aching muscles that threatened to call it a day. There were too many things needing her attention. The baby wasn't due for another few weeks, but she had a niggling suspicion it might come early. Though she'd gone to the hospital in Belize City for her prenatal visits, she was pretty much on her own on the island.

"Miguel, could you finish for me? I'm going to the office for a while."

"*Si, señora,* I will take care of it."

Reaching the office, she put in her code and went straight to the refrigerator. Rosita, as usual, had completely stocked it with cold drinks and healthy food. She quirked her lips at the choices. What she really wanted was chocolate.

Her walkie-talkie chirped with static, then Rafa's familiar voice harassed her once more. "You forgot to check in at ten. Are you okay?"

Dammit, his check-ins were becoming a pain in the butt. She clicked the speak button. "Aren't you supposed to be teaching bad things to military guys in the jungle?"

Her irritation made her sarcastic. She was fully aware of the good work Rafa and the others did by training men in jungle warfare. Still, she had qualms. Brandon had used those skills to save her and Rafa. She shouldn't be so disparaging.

"Good morning to you too, Doc."

"Sorry, I'm feeling very pregnant and overwhelmed by the work that needs doing. Rafa, I need an assistant."

"Isn't Miguel helping? I could send a couple of men over."

"No! Security is very important. I need a trained lab assistant."

Silence met her words, then Rafa's voice sounded. "We shouldn't discuss this over the mike. Tonight, we can figure something out."

The mike clicked off and she heaved a sigh. Gulping a large slug of fresh lemonade to cool her temper, she moved to her desk and the mountain of work. Jackson and Charlene would be back tomorrow. And that would be a tremendous relief. The woman Brandon had chosen to be her bodyguard had enormous potential as a worker and a friend.

She worked for an hour before the baby began to bounce up and down on her bladder. Standing, she experienced a wave of dizziness. Quickly, she sank back into the chair and pushed her head between her knees—or as close to her knees as she could with the large protruding bump in the middle. Vaguely, she noted the beeps of someone keying in a code. A stab of fear jerked her head up. Charlene was right. She was totally isolated out here.

The lock clicked open, and Rafa poked his head around the door.

"How did you get the code?" Her tone sharp, she swallowed before continuing. "Really, how *did* you get it?"

"I'm in charge now, so Jackson gave me the code. I

also have the codes to the nuclear football."

She smiled. Rafa could defuse any tense situation with his wit and dazzling smile. "You better not let Brandon know. He'd take you into custody himself."

She loved the easy banter with Rafa. When the two of them worked together in the Honduran jungle to rescue Brandon, his good cheer had kept her going. She'd been ready to give up, but not Rafa. He'd come up with a plan and then a second one. *SEALs never know when things might go wrong.* The remembered words perked her up.

"Tell me why you sounded so frazzled, Doc."

"I was so hot, then when I stood, I got very dizzy."

"And the look of panic on your face, just now?"

Behind his easy manner, Rafa was sharp as a tack. She wouldn't be able to fool him, so she went with honesty. "You frightened me. I thought Brandon and I were the only ones with the code to the office. Charlene was concerned by my isolation and the one code to the office. I guess her words made me aware of it myself."

"I'm sorry you were frightened. The three partners decided that certain secrets should be shared. It was for your safety." He took her glass and refilled it from the pitcher. "Here, rehydrate and rest a minute. After that—it's bedtime for you."

"I don't have time to lie in bed."

"You should know, doctors make the worst patients." He took out his cell and stepped outside the room.

Damn. As wonderful as this pregnancy was, it had its downside. People tended to order you around, and men got all puffed up and protective.

Rafa popped his head around the door. "Ready? I've

just gotten word that the supply boat brought a guest."

"Who?" Her heartbeat thundered. Could it be him?

"Don't go getting all excited. It isn't Brandon. It's his sister, Sandy. Brandon talked to her before he left."

Mira swallowed disappointment that it wasn't her husband. She perked up at the thought of Sandy. They could have so much fun, and she would be so helpful.

She took a quick look at the piles of papers and then at him. "I'm ready."

Later, Mira touched the brightly colored carousel pony dangling from the mobile over the crib. She'd been hard-pressed to keep Brandon from painting the nursery in camo colors. After much *discussion,* they'd settled on a pale green. The soft color looked cool, hinting at the rain forest surrounding the house. She hoped to accent the walls with bright touches of forest plants and animals. Thoughts of her husband stirred warring emotions in her chest. Anger got the upper hand and she turned from the crib and bent to pick up a box from the floor.

"Don't you dare," Sandy exclaimed. She entered the open door, deftly moving the box from Mira's reach. "Where do you want this?"

"Hi, Sandy. I'm trying to work off a little built-up steam. The nursery is nowhere near ready." She pointed to the changing table beneath the window.

"Well, I'm here to help. With the kids at the grandparents for two weeks, I've got nothing but free time."

Mira looked at the assortment of boxes and sighed. "We can start by unpacking the box by the door and continue from there." She wanted time to think, but Sandy's intrusion was for the best. Brandon had his reasons for leaving; she trusted him. The thought sent her mind back to Brandon's rescue eight months earlier.

Trust me. He'd spoken those words when she faced her worst fear. *I won't let you drown.* They'd submerged beneath the murky waters in the Mangrove swamp. The downdraft from the helicopter, bullets flying at her, and then an explosion.

"Are you all right?"

Sandy touched her arm, and Mira flashed back to the present, realized she was shaking, and allowed Sandy to help her to the chair.

"You're pale and clammy. Tell me what's wrong. I know you're upset because Brandon left on a special mission."

"It isn't the only thing bothering me. I'm worried about the research, and I'm nervous about the baby coming while he's away."

"That's enough to make anyone shake. I don't have any magic answers, but I have had children." She placed her palm on Mira's protruding belly. "From the feel of this, I'd say you're having Braxton-Hicks contractions."

Mira's brow furrowed at the words.

"Don't be alarmed," Sandy soothed. "They're perfectly natural."

"Right, they're normal the last month. I hadn't recognized them until you mentioned it. I've been tense off and on all day." She placed her hand over Sandy's on her tightened belly. "You've become such a good friend. I'm so glad we're family."

Sandy laughed and moved back. "Me too. Now, how about we start with that big box in the corner. It looks suspiciously like a glider rocker. I'll unpack it, and you try it out while directing me."

"All right. Could you get my laptop off the desk? I might as well get started finding an assistant. I've waited too long as it is."

Sandy cocked her head. "Are you sure about this? Surely one of the guys can find you one."

"Don't even go there. Left to the guys, my assistant would be a burly six foot six, a trained operative, and have a scientific IQ of fifty." She laughed at her own description. "I need someone PDQ, and I know just where to look." She turned on the computer and typed in the address for her old workplace. "There are always hungry post-grad students looking for jobs." She quickly posted the position in the jobs forum and shot off a short email to her former department head.

Chapter Twelve

Jackson rolled to his side and took in the sight and smell of Charlie. Images of them together, legs entwined, and bodies covered in sweat, filled his head. He took a deep breath to clear them. He fought the overwhelming urge to rouse her and make love again. Banking his passion, he rose, donned his pants, and looked out the window. Dark-gray clouds hung heavy in the morning sky as light rain broke the smooth surface of the calm water.

He grabbed his toolbox and slipped quietly from the plane. The door needed a better repair, and he wanted to check the propellers. Ignoring the rain, he moved to the nose and checked wires, hood fastenings, and hydraulics. With a deft hand he spun the blades. He tightened one of the screws to his satisfaction and with a grin patted the hood affectionately.

He used stealth to open the cockpit door and stow the toolbox without making too much noise. Thankfully, Charlene slept undisturbed.

He swam for half an hour and then left the water. The swim had done little to ease the turmoil raging in his chest and gut. He had to do something to tame his inner beast before returning to the plane, so he ran fast and hard. The sand crunched as he passed ghost crabs scuttling to find a hole to hide. He sympathized. If only he could curl up and hide in some hole.

"Dammit, get your head straight!" he bellowed at the seabirds following the water's edge. As they took flight, he stopped. He was no coward. Charlie wouldn't bite—unless he asked. No, it was time to face the piper. Turning his steps back toward the plane, he ran full-out, expending as much energy as possible. The confines of the plane made avoidance impossible. He'd have to endure her smell, accidental touches, and his own desire. Yep—it was going to be a fun trip home.

His steps slowed as he approached the plane. Charlene sat on the beach where they'd had their fire last night. Holding one cup in her hand, she nodded to the other cup on the log. "I hope it isn't cold. I wasn't sure how long you'd run."

He bent to take the cup, his senses reeling as her scent washed over him. Her musk mixed with a hint of their lovemaking nearly overwhelmed him. The coffee sloshed as he clenched his hand. Easing down to sit on the log, he took a deep swig of the coffee before answering. "I've missed my daily workouts. Running helps when I can't do my regular routine."

Charlene shifted on the sand and looked down at her hands. "Do you still train as hard as you did in the military?"

"Yes. We don't have the same resources as the SEALs. Constant training is a must, or someone could get killed."

"Not much has changed, then."

He tried to keep his voice even as he spoke, but this was an old argument, and it was time to end it. "It's my chosen job, *cher*. I can't imagine what I'd do without it. You've had a taste of it, and I know you liked it. If we take our relationship further, you must come to terms with the danger and chance of my being killed. Hell, I could just as easily get blown up in a building by some terrorist trying to make a point."

"What happens now?"

He heard the uncertainty in her voice but wasn't sure how to ease it. He'd chosen this path and intended to stay the course. Making a difference was something his *grandmère* had instilled in him as a small boy. *You might not make a million but strive to make a difference.*

"Now, we go back and do our jobs. Brandon is counting on both of us to keep things running."

Charlene poured the remains of her coffee onto the sand. "Right, let's go."

After closing the plane door, she tossed him a towel. "You're soaked. Why don't you change while I fix you some more coffee with cheese crackers? Your supply of staples is deplorable."

With a noncommittal grunt, Jackson moved to the back of the plane and stripped. She had her back to him, carefully averting her head as she made his breakfast. After last night, was she really embarrassed to see him naked? The idea intrigued him. Women got the strangest notions sometimes. *Grandmère* had told him as a young tadpole to be wary of women's moods. They change like the wind, and it could hail in the summer heat.

"Charlene?"

"Hmm?"

He took the few steps necessary to bring her back up close against him. "Are you being shy with me? You've seen me naked before in the daylight."

Red bloomed on her cheeks, and she tugged out of his hold. "That was different. We need to get back."

He sighed and began preparations to take off. The

engine buzzed as he sat at the controls, waiting as Charlene buckled in. *Dammit to hell. What had gone wrong?* She sat stiffly, eyes straight ahead while the muscles of her jaw clenched. He muttered a silent oath and throttled up. The plane lifted from the water like a giant seabird finding an air current. Jackson leveled the plane and checked his heading. One look at the fuel reserve made him swear. "Dammit, its worse than I thought. We'll never make it home without refueling."

"Is that a problem?"

"The only place where I can refuel is kind of sketchy." He didn't want to explain why, but knew she'd have questions. "I've stopped there in dire circumstances and barely gotten away with the plane and my life."

Charlene turned to face him. "Isn't there another option? There must be some tiny backwoods place with all the shoreline and islands."

"This is out of the way and secluded. If I try some of the others and they don't have fuel, we'll be stuck. This place might be rough, but it keeps plenty of fuel." At least he hoped they did. It wasn't like it was on the main shipping line. Nor did anyone question where their supplies came from.

Twenty minutes later, they landed in a seedy, backwater marina. Jackson touched down far away from the docks. It would give him time to re-con the place, while still having enough room to get out safely if the situation turned ugly. As many boats lined the docks as planes. All shared an illegal air—right down to no names or craft identifiers on the wings or tails. He could imagine this place in pirates' time.

"Under no circumstances are you to leave the plane. Stay in the back out of sight," Jackson said. "This place has more than a reputation for illegal activities. A woman like you would go for an easy hundred thousand on the black market."

"I can't believe you're stopping here." Charlene unbuckled her harness and moved to the back of the plane. "We could get killed for a little fuel."

Jackson fiddled with a few controls on the panel, then reached under his seat and pulled out a box. He took out his weapon and did a quick check of the clip. Grabbing an extra clip, he slid it into his pocket and tucked the gun into his belt at his back.

"Are you expecting World War Three?"

Jackson gave her a scowl. "The unexpected. It always happens."

"What do you pay these guys with? Do they accept a credit card?"

"Nope, cash only." He went to the center of the plane and pulled up a piece of the rubberized mat. Lifting the lid, he put in the combination on a small lock box.

Charlene gasped at the stacks of bills bundled into the mini safe. There were American, Belizean, and various Central American currencies. "You carry that much money all the time?"

"Usually more, but I haven't restocked since my last trip."

The plane jerked as it bumped against the wharf, and Charlene nearly fell.

Jackson closed the trap door and covered it. He put the cash inside a large cargo pocket in his pants and opened the door of the plane. No one was around. The place looked deserted. He cautiously stepped out and secured the plane. Normally he would lock the door with his surprise lock, but he might need to make a quick getaway.

He made his way to the terminal. Inside was a roar of noise and activity. Gaming machines lined one wall, and several patrons dropped coins and sipped drinks.

"Can I help you?"

Jackson froze at the gruff voice at his back. The hair on the back of his neck rose as he slowly turned. His hand itched to grab his gun, but he didn't want to start a gunfight in the middle of Roz's Drop In. A grizzled old man, dressed in shabby coveralls stood there. Just stood there.

A voice yelled across the bar, "Ferguson, stop. Haven't I told you a thousand times not to sneak up on Navy SEALs. They can kill you in a hundred different ways. You'd never have time to make a move. Now get outside and fuel up his plane."

Jackson looked at the woman who wore the scars of living a long and rough life. Skin mottled from too much sun, wrinkles on top of wrinkles on her face. Her voice told of too much booze and cigarettes. Her nails were painted red, like the rim of her eyes and her thickly painted lips.

"Thank you, ma'am. How much do I owe you for the fuel?"

"Come on over and have a drink. Let an old woman rest her eyes on something pretty."

"Navy SEALs and pretty are not in the same category," Jackson said as he eased an elbow on the bar. He turned sideways at the bar, keeping his back to the far wall. "How did you know?"

"It's the way you walk into a room. Your eyes—they look everywhere and see everything. They're killer eyes." The woman poured whiskey into a questionably clean glass and slid it down to him.

"You're very observant, as well," he said. "What were you?

]The woman smiled in a way only he and others like him understood. "I was a military courier for the Navy. Got into all kinds of situations that required more than delivering mail."

Jackson looked at her with respect. Women coverts were scarce. He lifted his glass and toasted, "To the Navy." They clicked glasses and swallowed the bourbon in one gulp.

Roz's voice dropped low. "There's a bunch of ruffians out back. They've been renting one of the rooms I have back there. They're stoned or drunk all the time. They've been talking about needing fast money. Keep an eye on that plane of yours and of course that gorgeous face."

She cackled with laughter, as if she'd been sharing a joke, not warning him that he was in danger. He raised his brow. "How much do I owe you?

"Three for the fuel and one for the warning."

Jackson paid her and moved away from the bar. The room had become quiet—too quiet. He scanned the faces and noted two new ones. The regulars moved away from them, and he knew he was looking at two of those so-called ruffians. He'd seen groups like this before and they worked in packs. That meant there would be others outside, trying for the plane.

"That's a nice plane you got out there, Mister. Do you mind if me and my buddies take a ride in it?"

Jackson studied the man. He was tall with oily, unkempt hair. Between the wiry build and gleam in his eyes, he knew this man liked to sample the product he sold. "I'm afraid I'm a little short on space. I just picked up a load of office supplies." Jackson edged closer to the door.

"That's all right, we don't mind a squeeze. Besides, without you, there'll be plenty of room."

Out of the corner of his eye, he caught movement. Another one of the gang was near the bar—behind him. He heard the snick of a gun cocking. He whirled to face the armed man. Just as he began one of his disarming moves, the gun flew from the man's hands—his blood spurting onto his shirt. He didn't ask who or how but kicked the second man in the gut followed by a double-handed blow to his head. The third man ran out the back door.

Jackson heard *Darlin's* engines start. Panic clutched his chest. Adrenaline rushed through his blood. Charlie was on the plane. Dammit. Why had this taken so long? Grabbing his gun from his back, he rushed out to the plane. The door was open, and his breath seized. Gun raised, he jumped through the door. Charlene sat in the pilot's seat.

"Charlie, what the hell are you doing in my seat?"

"I'm trying to save your ass. What do you mean, going into a place like that alone? For the record, how many were there?" She switched seats and began to buckle up.

Jackson quickly took her place in the pilot's seat and strapped in. "Three." A sharp metallic ping on the roof quickened his preparations. He cringed at the thought of his new paint job and put the plane in reverse. A sharp jerk bumped the plane against the dock. Damn! It was still tied to the dock.

"Charlie, you'll have to untie us. As soon as it's

loose, jump in and close the door." It nearly killed him to let her do this, but he had to control the plane for a quick take-off.

"Got it," she called on the way out.

Another ping quickened his pulse. When he heard Charlie's gun return fire, he was half out of his seat. When the plane lurched, he sat back down and listened for the back door to close. Moments later he heard the hatch close and Charlene moving forward.

"Go," she yelled.

Jackson backed enough to turn and pushed the throttle. Soon they lifted into the air. It took several minutes for him to notice how quiet she was. He jerked to take a look and his breath seized. She'd been wounded.

"Charlie! You've been shot."

"Thanks for noticing, now watch the sky. I don't think I can swim like this."

"How bad is it? Do I need to stop the bleeding?" His voice rose in pitch, and he recognized fear. He could take out six armed assailants with no sweat, but Charlie shot? All bets were off.

"Under your seat—get the first-aid box." His words came out gravelly, but he was back in control. "As soon as I get enough altitude, I'll put it on autopilot and fix you up."

"I'm fine. He only winged me. Though I must say, I'd rather not repeat the experience." Charlene tore her sleeve and caught some blood before it dropped onto the seat.

As Jackson's muscles tightened, he kept one eye on the altimeter, the other on Charlene. At ten-thousand feet, he flipped a switch and stood. Grabbing the medical kit, he opened it and pulled out the supplies. Before he thought twice and stopped himself, he pulled her down to smother her mouth with a harsh kiss.

"What was that for?" she asked.

"Don't ever scare me like that again." He pulled the sleeve away and discovered she'd been right. It was a flesh wound. He cleaned it, applied antiseptic, and put a large gauze pad over it. Feeling better, he returned to his seat.

"You do that a lot?" Charlene looked at him with serious eyes.

Jackson didn't need clarification of her meaning. His job and its risks always came between them. "We all know first-aid, but Rafa is the best. He's had special training."

"I'm glad you can take care of each other. When you're away…"

"Here, take these and close your eyes. You'll need the rest. When Mira gets hold of you, she'll be very thorough." He dropped the two ibuprofens into her hand.

When Charlene relaxed against the seat and closed her eyes, Jackson took the plane off autopilot and flew them home.

Chapter Thirteen

Charlene rubbed her palms over the armrest as the plane coasted to the dock. She studied Jackson's profile while he was busy with the plane. Part of her wanted to reach over and cover his face with kisses. The other part, the practical part, worried. They'd agreed Jackson would become part of Hope's life. How that would play out was yet to be seen.

He removed his earphones. "Rafa called. Everything and everyone is okay. He said to tell you that Mother Goose is fretful."

Charlene took a deep breath. Here she was, worrying about her own problems, when she had a job to do. The plane bumped the dock arm, specifically made for the plane. "I hope she's not overdoing things. She's very headstrong."

Jackson laughed and unbuckled his harness. He stood, hunching over in the plane's low-ceilinged cabin. "Doc is very strong. She'll come through things fine."

The door opened, and Charlene scooted past him, suddenly desperate for fresh air. She looked up to see Rafa standing at the door. His eyes were unreadable but brought about a tiny frisson of unease. He and Jackson were friends and she'd hurt him. What was going on behind his inscrutable gaze?

"Everything okay?" He took her hand and helped her onto the dock. "Doc is in puny form, and I'm glad to hand her over to your protection. Sandy has worked hard to distract her, but I think she misses you."

Warmth bloomed in her chest. It had been a long time since someone had cared about her. She'd avoided friendships and questions by keeping to herself. Her aunt was the extent of her company. Her alcoholic mother didn't count. She wasn't there even when she was. Lost in a drunken stupor most of the time, she'd cared little about what happened to Charlene or the baby.

She gave Rafa a strained smile. "I missed her, too."

"Come on, you two. Time's a wasting."

"Yes, boss," she said as Rafa gave him a mock salute. Jackson was back in charge.

Their arrival sparked a celebratory mood in the household. Mira smiled more, and Rosita added even more recipes to her baking repertoire.

****

Three nights later, the entire staff was present as Jackson had called a meeting for after dinner. Charlene immersed herself in the homey atmosphere, reveling in the scents and sounds. Dinner was served with colorful napkins, cheerful plates, and the table expanded to accommodate everyone. Glasses clinked, and cutlery scraped as the group enjoyed Rosita's bountiful spread.

Jackson sat across from her. "Pass the beans, please."

She looked up to see him watching her with one of his interrogating looks. "Er, sure."

She picked up the bowl and handed it to him. His fingers touched hers, sending a jolt of electricity down her arm and into her body. Heat suffused her face and her hand shook, causing some of the juice to slosh from the bowl onto the table. She dropped her hands, leaving the beans in Jackson's hands.

"You didn't burn yourself, did you?" Mira asked beside her. She took her napkin and wiped at the small puddle on the table.

Charlene turned her gaze to her friend, finding a knowing look on Mira's face. The heat deepened in her cheeks. Silence greeted her when she turned back to the table. Conversation had stopped and everyone looked in her direction. Across from her, Jackson stood, raising his glass to all.

"I called everyone together here tonight to share some news."

The table buzzed with murmurs as expectant looks flew in Jackson's direction. Something in Charlene's stomach took flight. What on earth was he up to? Shifting in her seat she shot him a sharp appraising look. He looked happy on the outside, but she saw something beneath the surface. Doubt and anger yes, but there was something she couldn't put her finger on. There was a time when she could read him like an open book, but she was rusty, and he'd become more adept at hiding his emotions.

****

"Don't keep us in suspense. What is it?" Mira asked.

Jackson made eye contact with each person at the table, finally letting his gaze rest on Charlene. He was a jumble of nerves. He'd decided to do this without discussing it with her. She'd be angry, of course, but he wanted the world to know. He wanted to solidify his child's presence in the world—make it seem real.

"I'm proud to inform you that I have a child." Gasps came from the group surrounding the table. Everyone tried to speak at once. The devil in him enjoyed the utter shock on Rafa's face. Mira looked smug, and Charlene—well, Charlene was pissed. "Please join me in welcoming Hope Favre into our happy family."

Glasses raised and clinked. He let his gaze rest on the stormy eyes across from him. They promised retribution, but he didn't care. Now, she would have to acknowledge their child to the world. He couldn't let her crawl back into her safe place and leave him out in the cold. He wanted her and his child in his life. He had no desire to be the kind of dad who sent checks and visited twice a year. He wanted the whole enchilada. Him, Charlene, and their baby girl—one happy family.

He took a large swallow of champagne. The bubbling liquid did little to cool the burning heat in his body. Anger bubbled beneath the surface, only to be overshadowed by his ardor. He'd had a single taste of what he'd thought gone forever. He didn't intend for it to be his last.

Rafa stood. "To Hope." He drained the contents of his glass, then turned to face Jackson. "I think I'm with the rest of the company in wanting to know more about this momentous occasion. Tell us more." He sat; his gaze fixed not on Jackson, but Charlene.

The table buzzed with questions as everyone reacted to his news and Rafa's demand. He cast a quick glance at Charlene's pale face and guilt squeezed his heart. Well, it was done now. Whether she accepted his blunt announcement or not, he was determined to make her his once more. By the look in her eye, he had his work cut out for him.

Mira spoke up. "This is wonderful news. When do we get to meet her?"

Charlie jerked, sloshing champagne onto the table.

"Careful, *cher*. This is good stuff. We don't want to waste it.

Her eyes flashed angry darts at him. "It's okay. There's plenty more. I need to talk to you, now," she hissed in a low whisper.

"No, you need to talk to them." He nodded at the group stare focused on them."

She swallowed and placed her glass on the table. "I'm sure you've all guessed by now. I'm Hope's mother. I'm not willing to speak about everything, but she'll be here when I think things are settled enough."

Beneath the table, he took her hand and squeezed it. It had taken courage to say the little she'd gotten out. He was torn between insisting she say more and pulling her into his arms and protecting her from all this attention. He did neither. With forced laughter he sat up straight. "Let's enjoy this great spread while it's hot. You did me proud, Rosita. This andouille dressing is to die for."

Chapter Fourteen

Charlene put the last plug into place and stepped back with a sigh. Done. The communications array was complete. Now, the Brigade had the ability to track all team members, and stay in contact with them, at anytime, anywhere. She had no doubt Brandon's new endeavor would be a great success. Three decorated ex-SEALs, and a loyal work force made its expansion a given.

She'd honed her skills both physically and mentally during her time with the combined military and civilian elite response team. There, she'd discovered her passion for organization and sharpshooting—and so much more. Jackson had been one of her instructors, and they'd broken all the rules. Impatiently she shook her head, ridding her mind of his image, and spoke into the mouthpiece. "Alpha-1 to Beta-1, come in."

Rafa's voice came across the com unit. "This is Beta-1. The clarity of this new system is phenomenal."

"For what you guys paid, it should do hula dances."

"If only."

Rafa's cool welcome had warmed a little since the night she'd arrived. Distrustful, like most ex-SEALs, he withheld himself from newcomers—especially those who had hurt his friend. She couldn't blame him but missed the teasing he used to indulge in with her. "I've configured the program to accommodate all island sectors. Each traveling unit will have their own code and channel."

"Great news. We've needed this—"

Loud, angry voices drowned out Rafa's words. Charlene listened closely, unable to discern Jackson's voice among the angry shouts.

"Charlie, I'll get back to you."

The link clicked off, leaving her to wonder at the argument going on in the background. The words had sounded clipped and urgent. A shiver of unease trickled down her spine. A thousand scenarios raced through her mind; none close to the reality of what could go wrong with military training. Weapons fire, heavy equipment, and testosterone-driven alpha men combined to create dangerous outcomes. Finished with the electronics, she wandered outside for some sun and fresh air.

From her position on the front veranda Charlene kicked the old rocker into a gentle rhythm. The glass of lemonade soothed her throat, raw from arguing with Jackson. Since the surprise party where he'd spilled her secrets, they only spoke in loud voices, if at all. She did her best to keep all communication strictly business. That was difficult on a tiny island with him as her boss.

The sound of tires on gravel alerted her. The jeep pulled to a stop with a screech of tires. Rafa sat behind the wheel with a thunderous expression on his face. A stranger who must have arrived on the weekly supply boat rode shotgun. Whoever he was, he looked hot, travel-worn, and disgruntled.

Stumbling from the jeep, the newcomer moved to the steps of the veranda while Rafa reversed sharply and took off with rocks flying up behind the wheels.

He walked toward her with his hand out and a wan

smile on his face. “Hello. I’m Devon Williams, the new assistant.”

Surprise, worry and irritation flashed through her. Her and Jackson’s argument a few minutes ago had centered around an assistant. As far as she knew, no one had been hired. Who the hell was this guy?

She automatically grasped his limp, sweaty hand. “Hi, I’m Charlene, secretary and all-around dogsbody. You name it, and Jackson has me do it. I’m just lucky I’m not good at soldier stuff, or he’d have me down with the men practicing.”

She knew she was chattering to cover her reaction to him. At about five foot seven inches, with balding hair, Devon wore baggy pants and a long-sleeved dress shirt that had been popular about fifteen years ago. His skin gleamed white in the heat of the afternoon. She saw lots of sunscreen in his future.

The front door opened with more force than necessary. Charlene had no doubt about the person’s identity or his mood. Rafa must have radioed Jackson before he’d driven two hundred feet. Jackson flashed an angry scowl at her before turning a polite look upon Devon. She wasn’t fooled. He could be very dangerous while still appearing genial.

“Mr. Williams, I’m Jackson Favre. While my partner is away, I’m the man in charge.”

Charlene didn’t need to see his sardonic smile to know that he’d heard every word the two of them had spoken on the porch. So, he’d taken to eavesdropping now, she mused.

“Charlene, be a dear and bring Mr. Williams and me some lemonade.”

Now, that wasn’t in her job description, but she

wasn't anyone's fool. She hastily headed for the kitchen. Jackson wasn't letting this man into the house without proper interrogation. She hurried toward the kitchen, fervently praying that Mira was still upstairs napping. Her hopes were dashed as she heard a delighted laugh bubbling through the kitchen door.

"Mira, you should have rested much longer," she admonished mildly and quirked her brow at Sandy.

The other woman gave a slight shrug. "I can't get her to listen either. She's nesting."

"I can't sleep until the baby comes. There's still so much to do. Was that Rafa who pulled up? I need to talk to him."

Charlene cringed. She'd have to tell her. "He just stopped by to drop someone off and went right back."

Excitement bloomed on Mira's face. "Someone's here? Who?"

"I'll let Jackson introduce you, I've got lemonade to prepare," Charlene snarked.

"No, *señorita*," Rosita said. "I have plenty prepared. Go with the *señora*. I will bring it out."

As Rosita took her only excuse, Charlene quickly followed Mira and Sandy out onto the veranda.

"Devon," Mira screeched and waddled over to give their guest a hug.

Devon Williams looked shocked. "Dr. Phelps, I had no idea you were pregnant. Congratulations." He gave her an awkward pat on the shoulder.

Charlene edged to stand behind the second rocker and backed into Jackson. She felt his muscles tighten at her touch. Was he still angry with her or at the situation before him? She couldn't tell. He'd gone into what she called his stealth mode. She couldn't read any expression except the one he wanted her to.

"Sit down, Doc." Jackson's voice softened on the nickname. "We'll get acquainted over some of Rosita's lemonade."

"Devon, you made it so quickly, I'm so glad. I desperately need help. My girth is slowing me down in my research."

Jackson frowned and leaned forward. "Did you engage Mr. Williams? That's my purview."

"If I left it to you or Rafa, I'd get an assistant when the baby turned three," Mira huffed. "And then he'd wear a uniform and be armed to the teeth."

"And your point is?" Jackson barked. Looking chagrined, he softened his tone. "Look, Brandon left me in charge of the safety of everyone on this island. He'd kill me if harm came to you. All new employees must be completed vetted. Are you forgetting why we must be so careful?" He stopped, though his face said he had lots more to say. He must have seen the hurt on Mira's face.

"Hey, I don't want to cause any trouble with anyone," Devon said. "I answered the ad because I worked with Dr. Phelps at the University."

"You're not a problem. You do good work, and I need help now," Mira said as she raised her chin toward Jackson.

Charlene decided to intervene before things got further out of hand. "Everyone has good points. Boss, how about you chat with Mr. Williams while—"

"Call me Devon. Everyone does."

"Okay, Devon. Mira and I will speak to Rosita then grab our things. We'll take you on a quick tour of the setup here before supper." If she didn't head Jackson off, Mira would be in tears.

"Wait just a damn minute," Jackson blurted.

Charlene raised a brow at him and turned to Mira. Her excitement was almost contagious.

"I can't wait to get Devon started on the project. We've got to have a celebration tonight. I'll see if we have something special in the larder." Mira headed off to the kitchen.

Charlene cast a sympathetic smile back at their guest. When Jackson intercepted the look, his brow twisted in a frown. She waved her fingers and sped after Mira. She didn't envy either Devon or Jackson. Both would be uncomfortable with the upcoming conversation. Mira would have the last word, though. How could Jackson say no when she desperately needed help?

****

Mira moved toward the kitchen as fast as any eight-and-a-half-month pregnant woman could. She wobbled a bit but moved quickly. "Rosita, we'll need something special for dinner."

Charlene noted the flush of color in her cheeks, and the sparkle in Mira's eyes warmed her heart. No matter how Devon came to be here, she could kiss him for that. A picture of the tic by his left eye formed in her mind. No, she would save her kisses. Besides, something about the man bugged her.

Leaving Mira deep in conversation with the cook, Charlene rushed up the stairs to her room. There, she changed her tank top to something with sleeves that could be loose at the waist. Snapping her Sig Sauer into its holster, she placed it at the small of her back. With a quick flick she smoothed her hair and headed downstairs.

"In my office."

Charlene started at Jackson's barked order.

"Now," he said when she hesitated.

"Do you want me to leave Mira alone with Devon?" She marveled at his control. By now, the old Jackson would have had Devon hanging from the nearest rafter, knife in one fist and a maniacal grin on his face.

"She'll be all right for the time it takes to say what I need to say."

The door shut behind her and Jackson grabbed her. His arms tightened around her, pulling her tightly against his body. Heat flashed through her as his hard arousal pressed against her belly. Was this the same man who had treated her like a pariah the last few days? At the thought, she stiffened, and he pushed her away.

Jackson turned and walked to the window and looked out. "Sorry, that's not why you're here."

Charlene fought to control her breathing and put a blank look on her face. "Then what is the problem?"

"Did you know Mira had put the ad on her former school's website?"

"No, I'm as shocked as you."

"I don't trust him."

Jackson's words mirrored her thoughts exactly. "He'll have to stay because she has to have help."

"I don't have to like it, but I agree. Tonight, do some research on him. Find out why Devon Williams is interested in Mira and her research."

Charlene turned to go but was stopped by his order. "Charlie, don't let him out of your sight."

"I won't," she responded. "It's just a feeling, but something is off about him."

She headed out to the porch only to find Rafa parked in the jeep out front. It seemed they were to have an escort. Rafa hopped out and came around to help Mira settle into the front seat. Charlene climbed into the back, and Devon joined her.

"Where do you want to start, Doc?" Rafa asked.

"Why the lab, of course." She turned around to face Devon. "It's small but well equipped. My husband indulges me with my toys."

"Why don't we save that for tomorrow?" Charlene said, hoping to keep Devon away from the lab until she could check him out. "If you two geeks get sidetracked in there, we'll never see the rest of the island," she added. "Besides, we dare not be late for the welcome dinner."

Mira made a face. "You're right. Tomorrow morning will be cooler, and we'll have all day to work."

Rafa gave a brief glance over his shoulder before slowing for the turn to the compound. "I think a few hours would be a little more realistic. Your research will still be here after the baby. Now you have some help—ease up a little."

Mira glared at Rafa. "I'm tired of everyone coddling me. I'm a doctor. I know how to take care of myself."

Rafa flashed his 'I'm adorable' grin as the jeep sped up. "Okay, Doc. You're the expert."

Charlene breathed a sigh of relief. Mira had a special place in her heart for Rafa. He'd saved her in the jungles of Honduras and helped her rescue Brandon from rebels hell-bent on his torture and execution. If she was snapping at him, then things were sliding to hell in a handbasket.

The road to the training complex was well maintained, and the jeep sped through the beautiful scenery. She turned to Devon. "How did you meet Dr. Falcon?"

A look of discomfort paled his skin tone even more than the milk-white shade it was. "Er," he hesitated then continued. "Dr. Falcon?"

Charlene noted his deflection of her question and decided to play along with his act of innocence. "I believe you know her as Dr. Phelps. She's married now to the head of this operation, Brandon Falcon."

"I had no idea. Congratulations," he murmured.

Mira twisted in her seat. "A lot has changed in my life." She patted her bulging girth. "I have only a few weeks left before the baby. I want to get you settled into the job before the baby arrives."

Charlene fixed Devon with a commanding stare. "So, you two worked together at Chapel Hill?"

"I was part of the research team who helped with her research. My part was merely educated labor. Dr. Phelps, er, Falcon, was far above my paygrade." He made a deprecating gesture with his hands. "I'm super excited to actually work closely with her."

Rafa caught her gaze in the rearview mirror. Yep, he didn't like the man either. Devon was so ingratiating, it left an oily feel in the back of her mouth.

"Here we are," Rafa said as he pulled up to the compound's guarded fence. "We can't go in just now. There's a drill in progress. Can't have innocents getting hurt."

He turned in his seat and spoke to Devon. "This is our training facility. Brandon's Brigade helps train men in jungle warfare." His stare turned into a warning look. "The compound is off-limits, Mr. Williams."

Mira shifted back around in her seat. "Don't worry, Devon. You'll be far too busy to wander around the island. Besides the beaches are fantastic. Much more interesting than this." Let's do a quick look at the lab, then I'll need to rest before dinner."

Charlene's gaze fixated on the very pregnant woman in the front. "Are you okay? We can do this tomorrow if you like."

"Just tired. I guess my excitement is wearing me out. Just a quick look at the lab, then we can go home."

Rafa eased the jeep into a U-turn and headed for the lab.

Devon leaned forward toward Mira. "Exactly what kind of work are you doing? Your ad said, botanical research. That's pretty broad."

"I brought a rare orchid back from Honduras." Mira's voice held a note of caution. "Your job will be to help with propagation and data collection. I'll go into specifics tomorrow."

Good. When it came to her precious orchid, Mira was no fool.

Rafa pulled into the small, graveled area outside the research facility. The building looked unimpressive, but the covered nursery area was huge. A young man carefully watered plants beneath the sun-screened roof covering. He looked up as they stopped and waved.

Mira returned his wave. "That's Manuel. He's the only help I have at the moment. He does the actual physical labor, like filling pots and watering. He's not much help with data collection, though. I'll introduce you tomorrow."

"Quite an efficient setup. I can't wait to start," Devon said.

"Security is tight, as you can expect. I don't want my research compromised," Mira said. "Charlene will brief you on that part. She's in charge of all security at the lab."

"You know I can be trusted with sensitive research. I'm just happy to be a part of your work," Devon murmured.

Rafa gave a pointed look at his watch. "If you're ready, I'll head back now."

"Sure. I'll have time to talk to Devon over dinner." Mira leaned her head back and rested it against the seat. "Let's go, Rafa."

The jeep lurched forward and headed home.

Chapter Fifteen

Jackson locked the door behind him. He needed to get a key for the office for Charlene. He didn't want to chance Devon wandering in and discovering secrets. Some of their clients were super careful about personal information. Some—could be dangerous if riled.

His nose led him to the kitchen where Rosita stirred something on the stove. "Smells great," he said.

The cook filled a spoon and handed him a taste. He sniffed it, then blew on it. He slipped the spoon into his mouth. A loud purr sounded in his throat. He flashed the woman a smile, then pressed his fingers to his lips. "*C'est bon.*"

"I thought you'd like it. I used the last of the andouille sausage in it. Mira said to pull out all the stops and put on a spread." Rosita grabbed two oven mitts and opened the oven. Sitting in its juices, a large Virginia ham sizzled, its scored fat glistening.

"I might ask more strangers to the island if we get food like this."

"*Señor* Jackson, you joke. I always fix good food for you."

He stepped away from the hot stove. "Rosita, I need you to do something for me."

"Anything, *señor*."

"Keep an eye on our guest. He bothers me, and I know very little about him."

Rosita gasped. “You are worried he may harm the *señora*?”

“I’m not exactly sure. Try to make your presence known when he’s alone with her. Better yet, don’t leave them alone if you can.”

That said, he left the kitchen and entered the living room in time to find Mira, Charlene, and Sandy descending the staircase. “You three look good enough to eat.”

“My, what big teeth you have, “Charlene murmured, causing Mira to giggle.

He stepped forward and clasped Mira’s hand as she took the last step. He took in the circles under her eyes and lines of fatigue on her face. She might look fragile, but he knew she had a backbone of steel. He had a special spot in his heart for the Doc.

Rosita walked by with a cart filled with food. “Dinner is ready.”

“Where’s Devon? “Mira asked.

As if conjured, the door from the veranda opened and their guest came in. An air of cigarette smoke clung to him as he moved forward.

Jackson led the way into the dining room and pulled out chairs for the women. He held on to Charlene’s chair a moment longer and whispered huskily, “You look lovely with your face glowing in the candlelight.”

Emotion thickened his accent as it always did, and he felt her responding quiver. Her color deepened and he lifted his head. God, what was he doing? His head had to remain clear. Too many lives depended upon him to let his heart and body rule his head. With an effort, he straightened, ignoring the hard flash of desire clawing at his body.

"How's your room, Devon?" Mira asked. "Do have everything you need?"

Her words helped to distract Jackson, and he moved to the head of the table. "If you are uncomfortable, I'm sure we can find better arrangements."

"I want him here in the house and not at the barracks." Mira's voice was firm. "We can discuss things while I'm sitting at night."

Before Jackson could speak, Devon said, "My room is quite adequate, Dr. Falcon. You have provided everything needed. The view from the window is amazing."

"You must call me, Mira."

"All right, Mira." Devon smiled.

Rosita served the first course, a seafood gumbo.

Jackson picked up his spoon and ate with relish. Pausing in between bites, he glanced at their guest. "Besides working at the university, what are your interests?"

Devon put down his spoon, then spoke. "I love plants. They're so uncomplicated. Living in North Carolina, I have to love NASCAR. I try to catch the races when I can."

"Which one is that? Charlene asked. "I know nothing about racing."

Jackson nodded imperceptibly. *Good girl.* Feed his ego and loosen his tongue. He stood and opened the red wine that sat on the sideboard. He hoped Devon was a drinker. Fine wine could smooth out conversations and allow him to probe without upsetting Mira. Clearly, she was a might touchy about her new assistant.

"NASCAR is racing with stock cars modified from their original form. It's pretty exciting—all the noises and smells of gas and rubber—smoking hot."

Jackson bent to fill Devon's glass. The man's excitement was apparent by his bright eyes and smell of arousal. Devon's gaze focused on Charlene. Jackson *accidentally* bumped the back of his chair. "Sorry," he said and quirked a brow at Charlene. Her face flashed her annoyance, and he moved past Mira, who was drinking water, to fill Sandy's glass.

The talk turned to plants. Jackson didn't know much about them, but he did know Rafa discovered the orchid Mira had been researching. She had used the only specimen he found to help save Brandon's life. Ever the scientist, she had written everything down about the orchid and what she'd done with it. The damn thing had not only saved his best friend's life, but it had also healed his shattered leg so he could walk. Later, on a quick return trip to Honduras, Rafa found more of the orchids and brought them back here.

By the time the ham and vegetables were served, Devon had consumed several glasses of wine. His voice became more excited as he turned to his hostess. "Could you tell me more about the research?" His eyes glittered and his face flushed. "I only know you're researching an orchid. Which one and what exactly are you looking for?"

Mira turned to face him. "When I was in Honduras, working for Doctors Without Borders, I encountered a unit of rebel soldiers. Brandon and Rafa rescued me. Brandon was wounded very badly and needed a miracle to survive." She paused and wiped the tears from her eyes before continuing. "My uncle, before he died, had researched a certain orchid, the Blue Spider Orchid, thought to have miraculous healing powers. I had some of his notes and described the plant to Rafa. He found the orchid for me. I'm trying to cultivate it and hopefully extract and identify the components that heal." She reached her hand out and covered Devon's. "This research is totally secret, and you must speak to no one about it."

Rosita rolled in coffee and peach cobbler with ice cream. Her appearance lightened the serious mood that had settled over the meal. By the time the table was cleared, the conversation turned to music as Mira popped in her favorite CD. A single violin, played by a master, filled the air with serenity and a little romance. As the orchestra joined in, everyone sat comfortably.

The front door banged open. Rafa barged into the room with urgency in every step.

"What's wrong?" Jackson asked as he diverted Rafa toward the veranda. "Let's not upset the ladies."

Once outside the doors, Rafa turned to Jackson. "We've got a situation down at the camp. I could use a little help."

Jackson patted his shoulder. "I'll be just a minute." He walked back into the living room. Everyone sat on the edge of their chairs, and the music had stopped. "I need to help Rafa with a few things." He caught Mira's anxious look. "No one is hurt, so don't worry. I'll be back later tonight." Before anyone could say anything, he left the room.

****

Later that night Charlene opened the door to the unlocked office with trepidation. It had been a long time before Jackson returned from the camp. Though she'd gone to bed, she hadn't slept. How could she when so much was going on? When he'd left, she oversaw security. She knew that several roaming guards constantly walked through the property at night, but worry was an old habit.

Jackson stopped his pacing and whirled on her. “I don’t like it. We know nothing about him. How did he even find out where we are?”

“Is everything all right at the camp?” she asked as she sank into one of the chairs.

“Nothing too serious. Too much testosterone and not enough sense. We sorted it out.”

She listened to his words but had her doubts. Rafa wasn’t a lightweight, and he didn’t panic. Something more happened than he was willing to share. “What did you and Rafa have to discuss that took so long?”

Jackson flashed her a glare. “Don’t get too inquisitive, *cher*.”

His shoulders visibly relaxed as she returned his stare. “How else am I to stay informed?”

“Smart ass,” he said with what sounded like affection. “Rafa and I both think something is fishy. When did Mira post the request for an assistant?”

“A week ago. Which was quick. He must have been glued to the computer to find the ad so quickly. Even so, Mira told me she hadn’t received any message or calls from him. Surely, Mr. Eye-twitchy Baggy-pants, doesn’t have the kahunas to show up without an invitation.”

Laughter erupted from Jackson’s chest. “You’ve got him pegged all right. Do you know if Mira posted an address or directions to the island? I can’t see her being that stupid.”

Anger burned in her stomach. “People do dumb things without being stupid. How the hell do you know what she’s going through? She’s pregnant, near term.

Her husband is away on a top-secret mission, and she's worried he'll be hurt or killed. Her research is important to more than just her. Who knows how many lives she'll save with her discoveries?"

Her anger dissipated as quickly as it rose. Jackson wasn't the problem. How could he know she'd gone through such similar stresses during the three years she'd hidden away?

Jackson slowly pulled out the chair at the end of the table and sat beside her. "*Cher*, look at me." His words were thick with Cajun and concern.

She wouldn't be able to hold it all back if he said anything else in his too-sexy voice. Tiny shivers skittered over her skin. When his fingers lifted her chin, his breath sucked in.

"*Mon pauvre bébé.*"

Unaware of the picture her face made with tears streaking her cheeks, Charlene bit back, "I'm not your baby."

He chuckled softly and pulled her head onto his shoulder. "If you were, I'd be jailed for my thoughts. You are a hell of a woman, not a child. You tie me up in knots with those tears." He sighed, kissed the top of her head, and pushed her back so her face looked up to his. "I know Mira is not stupid. What's really bothering you? Those words you threw at me were about you, not her."

Charlene wiped her tears with the back of her hand. "I chose my path. Yes, I was scared, lonely, and worried about you. With a little knowledge and some computer skills, a person can find out about SEALs while they are out of the country. I was able to find out through some connections that you were all right. I—" She paused. "I didn't know you were wounded, or I would have worried more."

"You must have some connections."

"I know some pretty powerful computer geeks."

"Hire one of them. We could use a brain in that department."

"I'm afraid I'll have to do. You can't afford their salary." Silence fell between them. She looked up into his eyes and said, "I'm sorry. I had good reasons for running away, but all actions have consequences. I was alone except for my aunt." She shivered. "I felt dirty and was terrified your career would be ruined if there was an investigation. We broke the rules, Jackson."

"You have no reason to feel ashamed! He forced you! My career should have been the least of your concerns." At her jerk, he softened his voice. "No matter how much we want it, the past can't be changed. We're going to be okay. With time and patience, mountains can be moved."

"Is that an old Cajun proverb?"

"Just something *grandmère* used to say to me. Look, it's late. Tomorrow, go with Mira to the lab. Use your laptop to research Devon while you guard Mira. I'll see what I can do from my end. Look up the ad and see exactly what it said. We can talk when she rests in the afternoon."

"Okay." She stood and moved toward the stairs. She wanted him to ask her to his room. Her ears strained to hear some word from him in the silence behind her. As she stepped onto the landing, she heard a faint, "*fais de beaux rêves.*" *Sweet dreams.*

Thinking she'd never fall asleep with her emotions all revved up, she changed and brushed her teeth. Her curiosity caught, she pulled out her laptop and looked up Devon Williams.

Chapter Sixteen

Devon removed the empty suitcase from the double bed and quickly surveyed the room. Rushing to shower and change, he'd had little time to study his surroundings before dinner. A bed, dresser, and easy chair were the only furnishings in the small bedroom. From the look of the old plantation house, you'd think they could have provided the hired help with something better. He pulled out his phone and eased down into the chair.

As soon as he sat, he wanted a *real* drink. The wine at dinner had been good, but the bottle of scotch he'd picked up before getting on the boat was calling his name. He pulled the bottle from the drawer and grabbed the covered glass off the nightstand. Three more hours before he needed to make contact. No way was he going to sit here and twiddle his thumbs. There wasn't even a TV, for Christ's sake. How did people stand it on this godforsaken island?

Drink in hand, he took the first swallow and grinned. Pretty soon, he'd be sipping drinks on a *civilized* tropical island. One with lots of bikini-clad women, umbrellas fluttering in the breeze, and beach waiters. No need to get up and fetch another drink. A simple wave of his hand would have one of the white-shirted young men hurrying to tend his needs. Maybe Tahiti. There were lots of beautiful women there.

The thought of women brought an image of Dr.

Falcon into his mind. Damn, she looked like a whale. A far cry from the slim Miss Hoity-toity from Chapel Hill. Always flitting around, her tight ass swishing as she watched everyone over the rims of her small dark-framed glasses. As if when she wasn't watching, everything would go to hell. He was a good horticulturist. Sure, she had lots of fancy letters behind her name, but he had a master's degree earned by hard work and scraping to make ends meet. She probably got her degrees on scholarship. Not that she'd ever said. She smiled and spoke of work-related issues and nothing personal.

He lifted the glass and emptied it in one large sip. Heat burned down his throat and warmed its way to his stomach. Tension eased from his body, and his mood mellowed. Once more he contemplated his new boss. He'd never expected to find her married to a former SEAL who ran some sort of paramilitary business. It would make things harder, but he could handle it. He would keep that nugget of information to himself. No use alarming his *friends* unnecessarily.

He poured himself another hefty drink and touched the screen of his phone. Dammit, he looked at the screen irritably. How was he expected to know the wi-fi password? Snorting in disgust, he scrolled through the apps until he found his game of solitaire. It was going to be a long night.

****

Jackson waited until Charlene closed the door, then sat down. He felt the burden of the responsibility Brandon had left him. Was he up to the task? He had always been more of a follower than a leader. He thought he had a handle on things, and then *wham*, Devon Williams blindsided him with his appearance. The assistant was an unknown element, and Jackson didn't like unknowns. Before their SEAL missions, they'd been briefed with the best intel good money could buy and spies could ferret out. The US military was nothing if not diligent. All T's crossed and I's dotted.

They were seriously going to need more staff. Charlene was good with computers but lacked the strategic training necessary for covert missions. Besides, she had more than enough on her plate. She'd been great at interceding with Devon during their 'talk' at dinner. Charm, he had, but nothing like what she could do with a smile and gentle questioning. Now, if he could keep his libido in check and not distract her, she'd manage to get the scoop on the new assistant.

A memory assaulted him. *He could smell her scent—feel the softness of her skin.* How was he going to cope with his responsibilities when she distracted him? Her eyes laughing up at him. Their time together had been short but—oh so sweet. He'd known it was wrong to pursue her—military regulations were very clear about such things. Her gutsy *I've got this* attitude had drawn him in. Courage and stamina were grueling for most soldiers, but she dove in and excelled, especially in marksmanship. Damn, he grinned, she even bested Brandon in a tournament. He was a trained sniper, so her win was a noteworthy achievement. Then—she disappeared.

Pain shot though his stomach, and his chest squeezed. She was gone—no word—nothing. He'd reacted with anger and despair—searching for her, demanding information from the civilian project. His perspective became skewed, and if Brandon had not taken him to task, reminding him of his job, he'd have lost his spot on the SEAL team. Moreover, he'd have lost hope.

Jackson shook himself to clear the nightmare of his memories. It was in the past—no way to change it. He'd assumed the worst. She was dead to him, so he got on with his life. In his heart was a hollow space filled with all his boyish dreams. He became a stone-hearted soldier—ready to die for his country.

Tired of painful memories, he turned out the light in the office and headed to bed.

****

Charlene walked silently down the hall, crossing to the other wing. Jackson's room was the last on the right. She knew she was making a mistake, but she had to talk to him. Still dressed for dinner, she walked quietly past the door to Devon's room, noting the light shining beneath. Using her laptop, which didn't have all the secret data resources of the Brigade's computer, she had gathered a little information on their guest. She would access those resources tomorrow and chat with a few tech friends she had made in college.

She tapped gently on Jackson's door. Heart racing, she waited for him to answer. Darn it, she was nervous. It was late at night, and this was his bedroom. This seemed more intimate than their lovemaking. Before she could change her mind, the door opened. She swallowed the gasp which crawled up her throat at his appearance. Damp from his shower, a pair of shorts clinging to his body, his heat engulfed her. His chest, with all its hard-earned muscle, dog tags nestled in the curly dark hairs, drew her eyes like a magnet. Heat stirred between her legs.

"Charlie?" he questioned huskily. "Is everything

okay?"

At the sound of his voice, she looked up. "I need to talk to you." Did those breathy words come from her? Those blazing eyes made it difficult to think.

Jackson's nostrils flared, his shoulders stiffened, and he stepped aside. "Come in. I thought you'd be fast asleep by now."

Her gaze darted around the room as she made a beeline for the chair. Surprised to see an air of homeyness to the room, she sat awkwardly in the easy chair. His room was large, with another office setup in the corner. Jackson had never been much for decorating, but she could see some of the personal touches he'd added. A framed photo of his *grandmère* sat on his bedside table. He'd always spoken of her with such love and admiration.

"Is this about our guest, or something more personal?"

"Business." She swallowed and wet her lips. "I've done a cursory check on our new assistant. I'll need the secure computers to dig deeper."

Jackson pulled the chair from the desk and turned it, so he straddled it backwards. "Anything interesting?"

Realizing he was only interested in information, Charlene relaxed at his tone. "He's like vanilla ice cream or unbuttered toast."

Jackson chuckled. "After tonight's delightful meal, that sounds pretty bland."

"His parents were bible-thumping Christians. His father was an overzealous minister who browbeat both Devon and his mother. After high school, he fought with his parents and left. He tried to enter the Navy and Air Force. Both turned him down."

Jackson rolled the desk chair back and forth. "That's interesting. I'd like to see his psych-eval."

Charlene dropped her eyes to the floor. "I'm a good computer tech, but that is above my pay grade. Those files aren't easy to access."

"I'll call in a few favors tomorrow. If he didn't pass his evals, he might be dangerous."

Playing the devil's advocate, Charlene said, "Maybe he was after the college benefits. He'd need a lot of money for both a BS and a master's. He'd need both to hold his position at the university."

"Any other insights?"

"Not just yet. I do know Mira needs help. Even if this guy is more than he says, we can keep a close watch and still allow him to help out."

Jackson stood. "All right, you stay on him. No matter what other duties you have, Mira's safety comes first."

Charlene stood and edged toward the door. "I'll see you in the morning. Good night."

She moved quickly. Not that she didn't trust him, she didn't trust herself.

Chapter Seventeen

The next morning, Charlene stood in the shade of the nursery, close enough to hear conversation between Mira and Devon, yet far enough away to give the two scientists room to move and work.

Mira walked between the flats of plants resting beneath the sun-tarp with Devon shadowing her. "These are the seedlings I cultured from the original orchid tissue," she said. "We need to transplant them and label them with their numerical designation."

Devon gently touched one of the leaves with something akin to avarice in his body language. "Where did you say you found the orchid?"

"I can't divulge the source. Security is something I take very seriously. Suffice it to say, there will be no more samples from the source. What I have here must survive, or once more the Blue Spider Orchid and its reputed healing properties will fade into legend."

Charlene noted the way Mira leaned against the table. It was a good thing Devon was here to relieve some of the workload. "Mira, why don't you let Manuel help Devon get started so that you can come inside where its cooler and work on data."

Mira shot Charlene a glance that was part thankful, and part irked. "If my body were in better shape, I'd have some smart-ass comment. However, I think your suggestion has merit." She handed the tablet to Devon.

"Manuel will show you the ropes. You're in charge of making sure all data is recorded accurately."

Devon glanced down at the program on the screen. "No problem. I worked with orchids research at UNO. Do you have your potting mixture prepared, or do you need me to do that as well?"

Mira touched Devon's arm lightly. "Bless you. Manuel has the formula. It's such a relief to have your help."

Charlene did her best not to hover as Mira waddled toward the door of the lab. At a guess, Mira had only days before she'd have to quit coming to the lab. She closed the door, welcoming the coolness and headed for the refrigerator. After pulling the pitcher of lemonade from the shelf, she snagged two glasses and sat at the small table. Then she grabbed a rolling stool to elevate Mira's legs. "You can't do this for much longer."

Mira took a swallow of the lemonade, rubbing the glass against her forehead. "I know, but I have to get Devon trained before I slow down."

"It has to be more than slowing down. You need to quit working on your feet." Charlene didn't like the reprimand in her tone.

Mira's feet dropped to the floor, and she gave Charlene a frown. "Don't you think I know that? I'm a doctor, remember?"

She'd never heard Mira speak so harshly. She swallowed some of the cool drink as the words hung in the air between them.

Mira reached out and took her hand. "I'm so sorry. I feel wretched about what I just said, and my body needs a rest. Forgive me?"

Charlene patted the hand that clung to hers. "I

remember being this cranky, and I didn't have nearly as much on my plate. No forgiveness is necessary. We'll enjoy our drink, and then you can instruct Devon some more. After that, you can take a nap. Deal?"

"Deal."

Charlene finished her drink and followed Mira back to the nursery.

****

After her break, Mira bent to a tiny orchid clinging to the strata *aka* bark. It looked healthy. Quickly, she scanned the label, notated the height, and described its appearance. After finishing, she stood and absently rubbed one fist into the small of her back. "So, is the old gang still sludging away at the institute?"

Devon looked up from his job of meticulously filling the prescribed soil mix into each individual pot and swiped a dirty hand across his forehead. "Whew," he said and stood. "It sure is a lot hotter here than I expected. Evangelina left. She got a great spot on an African research team. Then, she up and got herself pregnant so that plum of a job is long gone.

Mira ignored the disgruntled tone in Devon's voice. "That's wonderful for her. There'll always be more jobs. Having your first baby is an experience like no other. I hope she's well."

"I don't know," he said. "I haven't kept up. What exactly are you looking for in your orchids?" He pulled a bottle of water from his pocket and drank till it was empty.

There it was again, she thought. Devon mining for information. Maybe there was something to what Jackson and Rafa had to say. No. She was not going to question the ethics of her former co-worker. If he was going to be of any help to her, she had to trust him.

"I'm looking for medicinal uses of the plant. I haven't set my sights on any disease or cure. I'll just see what comes from the research." She wasn't about to tell him how the Blue Spider Orchid's properties had saved Brandon and his leg in Honduras. She knew exactly what she was looking for. "My main goal is to keep the plants alive and reproducing. I need a large population before I can sacrifice any single one to research. By the way, security protocol mandates that any rhizomes, leaves, and stems that are removed because of damage or disease must be incinerated. Miguel will show you where you can do it."

Devon smirked. "Can't have anything growing outside the fence."

"Right, I run a tight ship, and nothing leaves the premises without my permission."

Devon swiped his head against his sleeve and stared back at her. "Don't you trust me?"

"Don't feel bad. I trust only one man totally, and he'd track down and kill anyone who hurt me or my project."

He took a step back and nodded his head. "I read you loud and clear, Dr. Falcon."

Mira suppressed a smile at the look of fear in his eyes. He might not respect her as a woman or his boss, but her words about her husband brought him a reality check. Everything about Brandon was dangerous. The baby gave a ferocious kick, and she hitched her breath. "You're just like your dad, reminding me to stay focused."

Charlene came up beside her. "May I touch?" Her hand hung like a question in the air.

"Sure, maybe your hand will settle her. That kick was one of the worst yet."

"I think he's trying to tell mama he's ready for a nap." She placed her hand on the undulation of Mira's belly. "He's got a strong kick. That's good. Let's call it a day and go back to the house for a siesta."

"I know I need to lie down, but there's so much to do." She glanced around and then went to check the locks and lock the electronics.

"Mira needs to lie down, Devon," Charlene said. "Are you okay to work another hour or two with Manuel?"

"Sure, I'll walk back. It's close, right?"

"Not far, but too difficult for Mira. See you tonight."

Mira coded the door and called, "Thanks, Devon, Manuel."

Once in the jeep, Charlene buckled in, waiting for Mira to do the same. After lifting her face to the cooling breeze, Mira laughed when Charlene spun a tire.

Chapter Eighteen

Rafa carefully placed the minuscule missile into the PLX-3 launcher. This was one of the new models Brandon's Brigade had contracted to test. Like all new weapons, he treated it with care. After double-checking the coordinates on the laptop, he made sure it would land in the sea. Without warning, the device kicked into armed mode.

He managed to stop it, but the missile launched without the code. Hot gas from the backfire burned his flesh and blasted his arm with pain. The recoil pushed him backward, knocking him into one of the trainees. The bedlam that ensued sounded distant and not nearly as loud as it should. He faded in and out of consciousness.

The frightened trainee yelled, "Rafa! Medic, medic, we got a man down!"

Rafa felt his feet go out from beneath him just before his face-planted in the dirt. Everything had a surreal feel. His nerves on his shoulder, chest, and arm shrieked with pain. A yell ripped from his throat as hands touched him. Arms lifted him from behind, sending shock waves of pain through his shoulder. Someone lifted his legs. He swallowed hard to keep bile from rising in his throat.

"The missile?" he asked, batting at the arms holding him like a steel band. Big mistake. The arm was burned. Fire swept across his nerves and his breath quickened painfully. "Dammit, let go." No one was listening.

"Sorry, sir. You don't get any say in this."

Rafa struggled to place the voice. His head pounded and dizziness made his stomach roil. He stopped struggling. *Rayburn.* One of the Brits. Good man, so he wouldn't slam his fist into his face. The cold hardness of the exam table shocked him into awareness of his surroundings. Coolness touched his body and the sun no longer burned with its torch-like rays. He opened his eyes, frowning at the darkness. Quick hands sliced the remains of his shirt from his body. Chilled, he began to shake.

"He's going into shock. Get Dr. Falcon," Rayburn yelled.

****

Mira assessed Rafa's condition with quick, professional detachment, but the friend side cringed at the laceration on his shoulder and the angry burn on his neck. She smoothed the sheet and leaned in closer. "How's my second-best man?" Her question earned her the smile she expected. "What can you see?"

Rafa's grin widened and then in a pathetic voice he said, "I see a halo. Are you an angel?"

Tension eased from her shoulders as she returned his grin. "I'm far from one of those, as you well know. I hope the ladies won't shy away from your scars from this."

"Don't you know women love scars on men, Doc? They make little mewling sounds, then touch your booboos gently and give you kisses for comfort. Next, you get to tell them all the war stories and—"

"Tell me why I gave him drugs." Mira said to the room full of men. "I'll never get him to shut up, now. I need more room in here." Her stern gaze flashed across the bystanders before turning her back on the quiet exodus.

"I— feel sick…"

She got the emesis basin under his head just in time. Her lips twitched at Rafa's shocked expression when he moaned, "I never—get—sick." He heaved a few more times before lying back with a moan, eyes closed to the light. His eyes popped back open at her husky laugh.

"Sure, you do," she said. "I imagine it takes more than a little alcohol to turn you this green."

The door to the room jerked open behind her.

"How is he?" Jackson's voice bit out the questions as the air vibrated with his presence. "Is anyone else hurt?"

"He's the only one hurt, and he'll be fine," Mira soothed as much as informed him.

Jackson shook Rafa on his good shoulder." What the hell happened?" he barked at the now-sleeping patient. "Did he black out?"

"Back off, Jackson." Steel laced Mira's words. "He's in shock. I need to keep him sedated long enough to close his shoulder and cleanse his eyes with ophthalmic solution. Luckily, the backfire didn't burn his eyes, but the ejected gas propelled particulates into his eyes. I only pray he has no metal in there."

Jackson ceased shaking his friend and whirled to face Mira. "Are you saying he'll be blind?"

Mira grabbed Jackson's arm and pulled him outside the door. "He'll need to keep his eyes covered for a few days, but other than seeing a halo around my head, his sight seems good."

Jackson threw back his head and laughed." Rafa sees halos around all women's heads. If you've got everything you need here—" He paused, running a big hand through already harassed hair. "—I'll start on the FUBAR outside."

Mira's heart twisted with a pang. Jackson looked so strained. Normally, her happy-go-lucky Cajun would be ragging hard on Rafa. Of course, that would only be after assuring himself he was okay. Yep, he was feeling the weight of command. He headed out of the building. She heard him barking orders to the camp.

Chapter Nineteen

Three days after the mishap on the test range, Jackson exited the truck and walked toward the pier. Rafa's accident and recovery had slowed down the work progress. He'd spent most of his time at Beta-1, training the team as well as carrying out his multitude of other duties. He'd damn well punch Brandon if he mentioned taking charge again. It wasn't in his nature. He straightened as the supply boat pulled up against the dock. Two trainees secured the line as the boat bounced in the choppy water. The sun still shone, but they were in for a storm. They stood on the deck, duffel bags at their feet. Their stance and alert gazes gave them away for what they were, hardened soldiers.

Jackson turned his attention to the newest members of the Brigade's team. He let his gaze pass over each man, assessing their measure. They all came with great references, numerous decorations, and military training. Hell, he'd even worked with two of them once or twice. They weren't mercs. He wouldn't trust them if they were. All had good records upon leaving the military.

Standing tallest among them was Quentin Jameson, a former Army Ranger. No one knew the true story behind his departure from the elite group. He looked solid, standing six foot four, and broad shouldered. His blondish-brown hair blew in the breeze, giving him a casual relaxed pose. Jackson wasn't fooled. Like him, the other man was easygoing to a point. All hell broke loose when he was riled or in work mode. It was good to see him again. The men grabbed their duffels and jumped onto the jetty.

Jackson reached out and pumped Jameson's hand. "Damned good to see you. You healed that knee injury?"

Quentin flashed a grin. "A-okay. Not even a twinge when I run. Surprising since I'm an old man now." His voice held the soft drawl of the old South.

Jackson turned to the other four men. He offered a hand as each man introduced himself. Corbin Damons, ex SEAL; Wesley Jenkins, Marine Recon; Joaquim Hernandez, ex SEAL; and Tarek Ferguson, former Green Beret. They were an elite bunch, but he'd already read their files. He wanted to look each man in the eye and take his measure. Not one of them lowered their gaze, meeting his small challenge. Good. These men were the future of Brandon's Brigade. They would act as a solid five-man team, with either himself or Rafa taking the lead.

Jackson laughed and turned toward the men. "Throw your things in the back of the truck and hop in. We'll be in time for a late lunch. You're in for a treat. Rosita has been busy all morning frying and baking.

"I'm up for some island food," Wesley chimed in.

Quentin returned Wesley's fist bump. "You're always ready for food."

Jackson turned to face the men. I'll introduce you once we're inside the house, then we'll grab lunch. Afterward, we'll go to the barracks so you can settle in and clean up." He stepped onto the veranda followed by five pairs of clomping boots. "In a couple of weeks, you'll have to tone down the clomping. The doc is about to have a baby."

The door to the house opened, and Rosita met them with a big smile. She stepped back through the opening, allowing the group to enter. "My, you found some strapping young men. I hope I have enough to feed this lot."

While the men stood around, looking like a herd of bulls in a china shop, Jackson made the introductions. As he looked around, he recognized the many breakables on tables and shelves. "Is the doc around?"

"No, *señor*. She is resting upstairs. I took her a tray earlier. She says to welcome our guests, and she would be down for supper."

"Good. She needs to keep off her feet."

Rosita flitted around, straightening pillows. "She says *she's* the doctor. What can I do but try and see to her comfort?"

"She'll be fine, and you're doing a hell of a job keeping all of us on track. I appreciate your hard work."

Jackson turned back to the men. "I'll show you the office." He passed through the dining room and opened the door to the conference room. Charlene sat before an array of equipment and computers. "Gentlemen, this is Charlene. She oversees communications, problem solving, and secretarial. She wears a lot of hats. Be careful, gentlemen, she's armed and very dangerous. She's the only person to outshoot Brandon, your big boss."

****

Charlene's gaze fixed on the computer screen. The data she read quickened her breathing as her heart raced. Devon Williams was hiding secrets. When Brandon purchased the software to delve into the private lives of people, she'd been reticent, thinking it was a bit shady, but it had proved effective. Bank accounts, phone calls, and contacts scrolled down the page. She began her report.

The door pushed inward, bringing Jackson and a small herd of testosterone in the form of five men—and wow—they were certainly *male.* Training prompted her to close the screen before looking up at the men. Her heartbeat picked up as she met their gazes and blushed. She realized her mistake immediately. His face a cold mask, Jackson made a smart remark about her being armed and dangerous.

A swift spike of anger jabbed her brain, and she looked up into his face. "I think these gentlemen are more than capable of handling a little danger."

Hoots and laughter came from the five men.

"Don't encourage them, Charlie. They need to keep their minds on the job." His words were gruff and held an underlying warning.

The laughter and hoots stopped.

As fast as her anger came, it was gone. Irritating as it was to admit, Jackson was right. Flirtations and distractions could get men killed in their jobs. These men were highly trained but not infallible. She gave her *timid* smile and waved a hand. Turning back to her work, she ignored the rest of the tour only to sigh in relief when the men were gone.

When she heard Mira's voice in the main room, she saved and closed the file. As a matter of security, she hid the file in a selection of receipts from Rosita's kitchen budget. Now, that she knew Devon was a barracuda instead of an ordinary slimeball, she wouldn't put it past him to sneak in at night and try to read the files.

Hopefully, he wouldn't think the kitchen budget warranted a look. Jackson didn't want Devon to be alerted before he gathered enough evidence to convince Mira of his duplicity. Surely the passcodes and other security measures would stop anyone trying to gather information on the Brigade. The military secrets alone would be worth millions to the right party.

"Charlene?" Mira's voice called.

She shut down the computer and walked out to meet Brandon's wife. Charlene gave Mira a measuring glance and said, "You don't have to call out before entering. You're the boss' boss. You have access to anything."

"Yeah, but I also have manners. This way is more polite."

"How are you and the baby? Time to take you to the mainland yet?"

Mira plopped into the oversized easy chair. It was one of her favorite spots as Brandon used it often. She appeared distracted, and Charlene was more than a little worried. "You're not thinking of going back to work on the orchids today, are you?

"Of course. I don't plan to do more than check Devon's progress and then we'll bring him back in time to clean-up for dinner. It's so exciting to see all of Brandon's plans come to fruition. Did you meet the men? What are they like? Any charmers in the bunch?"

"Yes, hot, and I don't know. Jackson gave them a whirlwind tour and left within five minutes."

"Did you say they were hot? Charlene, you're blushing. Now, I can't wait for supper."

"Leave it to you to pick up on the one word. You better be careful. Brandon will castrate them if they smile at you."

Mira laughed, then caught her abdomen. "Shh, it's okay."

She talked to the baby as if it was in her lap and not her womb. Charlene felt tugs at her own womb. She missed Hope so much. Would she and Jackson work things out? A tug of war between parents wasn't what she wanted. Jackson had just as much right to Hope as she did. Every time she looked into the little girl's eyes, she saw him.

"Charlene?" Mira's voice brought her back to the moment.

Mira struggled to hoist herself out of the chair. "You were miles away. I asked if you were ready to go the lab? The heat will be the same regardless of when we leave."

Charlene jumped up, aghast she'd been caught daydreaming. "I'm ready when you are. I think I should drive. You look tired."

"*I'm* the doctor, remember?"

"You'd never let me forget that."

Mira shuffled toward the stairs and the tiny bathroom beneath. "Smart-ass. You've been around the guys a few days, and you already sound like them.

"Just trying to fit in. I'll get the jeep."

Chapter Twenty

Jackson's gaze swung from one face to another in the group of military elites. Until now, Rafa had led the squad and prepared the missions. Now, it was his turn. He'd made the introductions and stood before the group. How did Rafa handle newcomers? Brandon had said to train them hard and fast.

"Gentlemen. Welcome to Brandon's Brigade. Your presence here today attests to your skills and courage. We at the Brigade will treat you with respect. You will be housed in the annex where all the rooms are private. You'll take your meals at the mess hall unless invited to dine with the family. Your meals will be far superior to any chow in the armed forces. We expect great things and pay and house accordingly. Tonight, you'll dine at the house and then I have a little surprise for your first day. Clean up and settle in. Tag a jeep and be at the house at six o'clock."

Jackson jumped into the jeep, starting the engine immediately. As he drove away from the camp, he decided to run by the research facility to check on things. His neck had been tingling all day, wondering what that little weasel was up to. He wished he had the personnel to give Mira some extra help. They would have to pass their security check and that was tight. The importance of the Brigade's training program and the sensitivity and secrecy of Mira's work made it hard to get personnel.

Most didn't want to live as isolated and regimented as they were.

As he turned the curve, he saw Mira climbing from the jeep. Her movements were getting slower, and she looked tired all the time. Couldn't she rest for a few days and let *what's-his-face* do the work? He was a trained researcher. His gut clenched. He didn't trust the bastard with Mira or her orchid secrets.

Mira's feet touched the ground, but she clung to the chicken bar for support. Jackson hurried over and put an arm around her, taking some of the weight off her legs. His concern ratcheted up when he saw how swollen they were. "Hey, *cher*. When are you going to get rid of that stiff-necked husband of yours and get you a Cajun man?"

Mira laughed and leaned her head against Jackson's chest. Sobering, she asked, "When will he come home?"

"He didn't tell me. He only said it was personal. Someone he cares for must need help. That's the only reason I can think of for him to leave you just now."

Thank goodness it was all the truth as he knew it. Brandon had been thinking ahead. He had known Mira would tug at a thread until it loosened. Glad that he didn't have to lie, Jackson patted Mira's hand. Slowly, they went into the facility.

"I don't care what she said. I need access to her files." Devin's whiney voice raised in irritation. "Move out of the way."

Jackson shifted Mira behind him as Charlene stepped up beside him. She pulled her gun from the back holster, eliciting a screech from Mira. They turned the corner and saw Miguel blocking Mira's office door while Devon continued to issue threats.

Charlene's high-pitched whistle brought instant

silence. Devon turned; his already-flushed face deepened in color. "I can explain." His words jerked out between stiff lips.

Jackson advanced one menacing step.

"Wait. Everyone just calm down." Mira moved forward, parting Charlene and Jackson. "What's the meaning of this, Devon? I gave you all the access you need to do the work."

"Yes, but I need the premise and the background, or my work won't be complete." His words were jerky and laced with a strong shot of anger.

"That's not your responsibility. I need you to handle the data and details. I'll do the research and analysis." Mira spoke sharply, becoming quite agitated.

Jackson intercepted Charlene's gestures and quickly swooped in and picked Mira up, placing her on a chair by the desk.

"Stop it, Jackson. I'm fine."

"Sure, you are, Doc. Those ankles are about to pop, and what's that red line running up your leg?"

Mira looked down and grimaced. "Damn, I've been so busy, I hadn't realized they were this bad."

Charlene shoved a stool over and gently lifted Mira's feet onto the seat. "Relax while I get you something cold to drink."

Jackson edged closer to Devon, giving him his *cold-eyed, you're dead* look. It never failed to put the fear of God into whomever happened to be unlucky enough to be on the receiving end.

The man gulped, then straightened. "I have a right to know. Partners should share."

Jackson moved to block Mira from Devon's view. "Mira has only one partner, and it's definitely not you.

You're only a lab rat; don't go reaching for the stars."

"Miguel?" Mira leaned to the side, trying to see around Jackson.

"*Si, señora*?"

"There's a storm brewing out at sea, likely due tonight. We need to prepare."

"*Si, señora* Mira. I will get right on it."

After Miguel had turned and left to his assignment, Mira turned on Devon. "If you still want a job, get your butt in gear and help batten down the hatches. My research will be for naught if I lose all my specimens."

Jackson smiled. He'd forgotten how formidable Doc could be. He should have known she would keep her eyes wide open when going into any situation. She and Rafa had worked together to rescue Brandon. She'd once walked into danger and strafed a rebel camp with a machine gun, all the while worried about how ill her husband was.

"Charlene, why don't you take Mira home?" he said. "I'll stay and make sure the lockdown is completed."

"No!" Mira protested. "I have to oversee the work, and I have backups to make."

"You're going to make yourself sick." Jackson admonished.

Charlene handed Mira a glass of lemonade. "I'll watch her for one hour. Then she's going home to rest."

"You can't coddle me." Mira said in exasperation. "I have work to do."

Charlene placed a hand on Mira's shoulder. "You do indeed. One part of that job is incubating your baby. If you overdo you could harm it."

Mira's face paled. "I'm sorry. I'm being an idiot. Let me do the backups and gather my files. I'll do the rest tomorrow."

Jackson winked. "That's right, Doc. There's plenty of time."

Chapter Twenty-one

Later that night, Charlene tucked her gun into her holster. With six trained veterans at the table, she would hardly need it, though Brandon's words ran through her mind. *She's my reason for living. Take extra care with her.*

So, she'd wear the gun and take no chances.

The wonderful aroma of cooking spices wafted up the stairs as she made her way down. The room was crowded. Mira held court in the easy chair while the five newcomers sat or stood, drinks in hand. Sandy sipped her wine while Jackson played bartender. Devon sat nursing what looked to be his third or fourth drink. His eyes were glazed, and his cheeks showed the ruddiness of intoxication. She was very surprised Jackson allowed him that much to drink. She stepped into the room and noticed that all male attention was focused her way. They all stood as she walked forward, and one vacated his seat for her. From the files, she remembered this face and name. Quentin Jameson. She might have known he'd be a gentleman. From her research on him he seemed the type.

"Thanks, Quentin."

"Glad to be of service, ma'am." His voice came out deep and gravelly.

A tingle of awareness shivered down her spine. At that exact moment, Jackson handed her a drink. She didn't miss his sharp look or his tenseness as his fingers touched hers. He was seriously pissed. She hadn't done anything wrong and refused to act ashamed. It wasn't like she was encouraging the men to look at her. They were men!

Before she could take a sip of her drink, Rosita came into the room and announced dinner. A firm hand settled at the base of her spine and urged her forward. She recognized male territoriality and fumed that Jackson would treat her so. He was telling all the men to back off and stay clear. When he steered her to the seat on the right hand of the head of the table, she sighed. Resigned to enduring a meal filled with male posturing, she looked up in surprise when Quentin sat beside her. Mira sat opposite Jackson at the other end of the table with Devon to her right. Rafa came in late and sat beside Tarek.

"Rosita, you've out done yourself." Jackson took the lid off the soup tureen and groaned. "Men, you're in for a treat. This is gumbo, a southern tradition that Rosita indulges me with. The sausage is andouille from the bayous of Louisiana.

Charlene took a portion of the gumbo and passed it on. She had her eyes on the platter of jerk chicken. Jamaican in origin, it was served throughout the Caribbean, Central America, and any of the islands. She watched as the hungry men filled their plates to overflowing.

Jackson took a biscuit and passed the basket. "It's good to see you up and around, Rafa. What's the prognosis?"

"Doc says I can go back to work tomorrow with some limitations. As nice as the house is, I can't wait to get back to work."

Mira patted Rafa's hand. "Don't let him do any lifting yet. His shoulder needs more time to heal."

Everyone continued to dine on Rosita's feast. Tamales, meat pies, fried tortillas, beans, and a host of relish dishes and breads completed the menu. By the time dessert arrived, along with Brandon's own brand of coffee, everyone was pushing back from the table and talking. Devon said nothing. He might have been trying to stay under everyone's radar, but anger marred his face as he drank the dinner wine like it was water.

Too bad. Given his earlier behavior at the research facility, this group had a long memory and very sophisticated radar.

"I'm sure Jackson will appreciate the extra help." Charlene sipped the delicious coffee. Brandon had a thing for coffee and now owned his own coffee plantation.

Jackson looked up and down the length of the table. "This is a turning point for the Brigade. Tomorrow, we train fast and furious. There's activity in the tropics. We'll have to keep an eye on that while doing our regular jobs. Are we ready for tonight, Rafa?"

"What about the weather?" Rafa asked.

"They don't get a choice for weather on ops. They'll train tonight as planned."

Mira set down her fork. "They've just got here. Surely it can wait until tomorrow."

"No, they have to adjust quickly," Jackson stated firmly. "We won't be using live ammo on this first outing."

"Hey, Doc, don't worry none," Rafa said with a laugh. "These are big guys. We're just going for a little run. They haven't seen our jungle yet. I'll give them a little tour."

The five men groaned.

Devon stood, a little unsteady, but looked able to walk on his own. He said a quick good night and left.

Charlene's gaze met Jackson's. They were both watching Devon as he climbed the stairs. Too bad she didn't have any robotic flies. She'd send one to his room in a heartbeat. He was up to something, and she needed to figure out what it was. Unfortunately, the closet thing they had was the next-generation Hornet. A thermal imaging drone with a mini camera. It was too big for house use.

Within minutes, the storm blew in, just as predicted, but with winds higher than promised. Jackson stood; the others followed suit. "All right, men, we'll skip the jungle tonight. I'll let you run home instead. Rafa, give them some light and direction."

The skies opened up just as the men reached the veranda. Taking their new boss at his word, they began to run. Rafa turned around and yelled at Jackson, "You're getting soft, old man."

"One year older doesn't make me an old man, just wiser."

Rafa's reply was lost in the sounds of the oncoming storm.

Chapter Twenty-Two

Two days later, Rosita bustled into the kitchen. "*Señora* Falcon, the phone is for you."

Mira sat, sipping her decaf coffee and pulling apart a sticky bun. "Who is it?"

She couldn't imagine who would call at this hour. Her heart began to race as visions of Brandon hurt or dead filled her head. No! She would have felt it. Calming herself with that thought, she rose and went to the phone. "Hello," she said while her heart lodged in her throat.

Several heartbeats passed before Devon spoke. "Mira, I'm at the lab. I think you should get down here. There's something killing the plants."

Shock, dismay, and panic vied for top position in her mind. "What is it? How bad—?"

Devon cut her off. "Bad enough. I don't know what it is, and I have no idea what to do."

"I'll be right there. Don't touch the orchids until I see them." She hung up and turned to Rosita. "I have to go to the lab. The orchids are dying."

"But Charlene is at the camp. She had a package to deliver."

"I don't have time to wait. When she returns, tell her what's happened."

"But *Señora—*"

"It can't wait. I have to leave now."

Mira went directly to the closet by the door and

grabbed a set of jeep keys. Thankfully, there were numerous jeeps in the shed, and she quickly had the vehicle on the track to the lab. Her heart raced as she bounced over bumps. What could have gone wrong? A trickle of unease skittered down her spine.

Could Devon have—no—he was a professional. He wouldn't deliberately damage her research. She slammed on the brakes. "Sorry," she apologized to the baby who kicked after her belly bumped the steering wheel. Her imagination was creative, and she had gone through several scenarios by the time she reached the lab. Her fingers fumbled as she put in the code, so she had to start over. This time she was careful—the failsafe froze the lock at the third try.

"Mira?" Devon's voice came from the seedling section.

She hurried forward but stopped when she saw Devon calmly watering the plants. "I said not to touch the orchids. What are you doing?"

"Just watering as per schedule."

Mira moved slowly toward him. "Show me the affected plants."

"Why won't you show me your research? I've paid my dues, and it's time I earned something back."

"I owe you nothing." She moved closer. "You've just started as my assistant."

"That's always the answer. Who does the bulk of the work around here? Me!" he whined.

"Whatever do you mean? You worked for me as an assistant at Chapel Hill. Why should this be different?"

"Chapel Hill. There you were, Miss Hoity-toity, Doctor Phelps, looking down on everyone from your lofty aerie, only coming down to take the credit."

Mira was beginning to worry. Devon sounded mad. "I'm sorry you felt that way, but—"

"I've given you enough time to trust me." He pulled a weapon from his pocket and waved it at her. "Now, we do it my way."

Mira froze. All words fled as fear for her baby tore through her body. "Devon." She could only get the one word between her stiffened lips.

"What's wrong, Doctor Falcon? Nothing to say?" Devon waved the gun in front of her face.

She had to stall. Charlene would be coming soon. "What do you want me to say?"

"Only what I've said all along. I want your research. For once, I'll take the credit."

"You're on an island with a hundred trained men. Where will you go?"

"Don't worry your pretty head about that. I have friends coming to get me."

She grabbed her stomach and bent over. "Who do you mean? Brandon will kill you."

"I don't think your SEAL husband will say a word. You're going with me."

"I need to sit. The baby's pressing down."

Devon frowned but pointed the gun at the office. "You can sit in the office. When your little bodyguard gets here, we'll finish our discussion."

Mira jerked her head up.

"Don't think I didn't notice the gun she carries. I'll disarm her and signal for my friends."

"How did you get into the lab? It was locked."

Devon patted his pocket. "A jammer and a code breaker. Surprising what you can get on the black market these days. Your code was rather simple."

Mira shifted, trying for comfort in the rolling chair. "How did you know about the job before I posted it?"

"I wondered if you'd notice." He moved to lean against the sink. "I read about your discovery, snooped into a few files, and found your letter. The rest was easy. I knew you couldn't turn away help while you were so pregnant."

"You knew? How? This island and its purpose are classified."

"How the hell can you classify an island? Besides, the locals were more than happy to fill in a few details once the booze started flowing. My contacts have access to lots of information."

"Who—"

The outer door banged.

Mira's head jerked up "She doesn't have the code."

Devon laughed. "Not very smart, Doctor. What if you were in danger? She couldn't get to you."

Mira noted the color in his cheeks and the glazed eyes. She suspected he was high on something. It didn't matter. What he was doing was very wrong. If he hurt her or the baby, he was a dead man. Brandon would hunt him down, whatever hole he crawled into.

"I'm going to leave you in the office. If you yell out to warn her, I'll put a bullet in her head."

The pounding came again.

****

Devon shut the office and moved to the outer door. He held the gun in his left hand and yanked hard on the knob with his right. Off balance, Charlene tumbled through the opening. Before she had time to right herself, he brought his gun down on her head. He didn't trust her. She not only carried a gun, but he'd also learned the other night, she was a sharpshooter. Too bad, he liked her. But there'd be plenty of women where he was going. He'd have enough money to buy any one of them. A thrill of power surged through his veins. It felt damn good to be in charge.

"Devon, is she okay?" Mira's voice came through the office door.

"I told you to be quiet or I'd shoot her." He yanked open the door to her office. "Shall I show you just how willing I am to get this job done? A little blood might be more convincing."

Mira jerked back in her chair. "Please don't hurt her. She's a stranger. Whatever beef you have it's with me and not her.

"You got that part right." He grabbed Charlene's arms and dragged her into the office. As it is, I have plans for Charlene. Not nice ones, but plans."

Devon left Charlene in a heap on the floor and pulled out his phone. He punched his contact's number and broke into a big grin. Excitement rushed through him as he thought about the prize at the end of the game. "I've got both women. How long will it take to get here? Fifteen's good."

He pocketed his phone and pulled a roll of cord from his other pocket. He tied up Charlene first, and then Mira. When he pulled out the bandanas, Mira protested, "Please. I can't wear a gag. It will compromise my breathing and harm the baby. I won't scream, I promise."

He gave her a deliberating look and then bent to tie the bandana around Charlene's mouth. He really didn't want to hurt the doctor or the kid, but his contact insisted. He'd wait until they were here.

"Could I please check on Charlene?" Mira begged.

"She's been out for a long time. She could suffer a brain hemorrhage.

"You couldn't help her now anyway. My friends will be here in about twelve minutes."

"I could check her breathing and heart rate. A dead hostage won't do you much good."

He studied her for a moment then helped her up but didn't untie her hands. As frazzled and pregnant as she looked, there'd be no way she could stop him. He watched her carefully as she felt Charlene's pulse, then put her ear to her back.

Charlene stirred when Mira touched the corner of her eyes. "She's coming around. That's good. She still might have a concussion." Charlene jerked. Mira stilled her head from moving. "Shh, you could have a concussion. Lie still and let me check your eyes." Don't try to talk."

"I'll shoot you if you put up a fuss," he warned. "It's going to be rough enough without a bullet wound." Devon placed the barrel of the gun against Charlene's forehead. "You going to cooperate or not? Mira might need some help, so I hope you'll agree."

After Charlene nodded, Devon moved to the outer door and looked out. The wind had picked up and brought the sounds of a helicopter. It was loud, like surround sound in the movie theaters. He turned and pulled Charlene from the floor.

Staggering under her weight, he put her in the back of the jeep beside a large plastic container. His prize, besides the money of course. He smiled at Charlene when she threw a malevolent look at him. Mira struggled to walk, and he went back to help her into the jeep. Quickly, he jumped in and started off.

Chapter Twenty-Three

Charlene felt like an avalanche had fallen on her head—though not nearly as cool. She was both dizzy and nauseous. And damn that smile. She'd love to smack it off Devon's face. She forced herself to stop shaking her head to clear it because each move sent pain spearing from ear to ear.

Her first thought was of Mira. Jerking her head up, she saw Devon shove Mira into the seat and slam the door. Charlene resented the fact a wimp like Devon had gotten the better of her. She'd suspected he was slime but hadn't expected him to suddenly develop intelligence. No—it had to be desperation. Any animal could turn vicious when cornered. Before Mira or the baby were harmed, she'd somehow get the upper hand and smash his insignificant face into peanut butter.

She jerked against the side of the jeep as they careened over bumps and turns taken too fast. Devon was wasting no time getting to his friends. As they rounded the bend, the jeep braked hard. Sitting in the open yard was an oversized helicopter. Like a giant steel bird, it sat with its rotors spinning and engines growling. Guns were mounted on the sides of the craft along with two ATLs, air to land missiles. Charlene swallowed hard. Whoever Devon's friends were, they had lots of money. Struggling with her tied hands, she frantically wrangled the cord, tearing her skin with no success.

She flashed a look at Mira and saw the dramatic change in her condition. She breathed in quick pants, shielding her face from the windblown sand. Bleached of all color, her face was blank, and her shoulders sagged.

"Devon, Mira needs help." Her words muffled against the gag as worry filled her.

He turned just as Mira slumped against the seat, her head lolling to the side. "Shit." He jumped from the jeep and went to Mira's side. "What do I do?"

Charlene leaned forward and called to Mira. No response. Alarm prickled her nerve endings. Dammit, she needed to get to her. Devon patted her wrists to no avail. She looked to her left just as four armed men jumped from the copter and sprinted toward the jeep. The metallic taste of fear flooded her mouth. These men were the real McCoy.

Bandoleros draped their shoulders, and high-powered automated weapons rested confidently in their hands. They surrounded the jeep. Without breaking stride, the closest man grabbed Charlene and pulled her from the jeep. She tried to shield her face, but her arms were jerked down. She was half-led, half-dragged to the copter. Strong arms reached down and pulled her up, then shoved her to the floor. The vibrations from the floor, fumes of diesel fuel, and the smell of sweat assaulted her senses. Heat and unwashed bodies combined to make her gag. The sound of gunshots ripped a scream from her throat.

His fist plowed into her face. "Shut up, bitch!"

Pain warred with fear as she fell to the floor and sank into blackness.

****

Mira's heart raced when she heard the loud noise of the chopper. The sound brought back memories of her and Brandon trapped in the mangrove swamp. Her fear of water—submerging beneath the murky depths. The sound of gunfire and bullets slicing through the water. The *whoop, whoop* of the blades rotating pounded in her head like a heartbeat.

Other sounds penetrated her darkness. Men speaking Spanish. She recognized the words, but something bothered her. The dialect was familiar. With a gasp she remembered—Honduran. Struggling to remain awake she took note of the four men with guns.

"You weren't supposed to harm the pregnant one. That's going to cost you."

Devon pulled himself up straight. Still, he lacked the height of the powerfully muscled commando before him. "She's all right, and I didn't hurt her. She's just in shock. The bitch never expected me to do something like this in a million years. I bet she's wet her pants."

Mira could only stare as the man fingered his weapon. Devon was stupid to challenge such a dangerous man. "See," he said, "her eyes are open. No problem—no big deal. Now, where's my money?

Two of the men met each other's glances with questioning looks. Finally, the one speaking to Devon shrugged. "You are a greedy little water rat with no loyalty to your friends."

"Wait just a minute. We have a deal, and I've done my part. You wouldn't have been able to just waltz in here without me. I cleared the way—earned her trust."

"You are correct, *Señor* Williams. You have done an excellent job. In fact, our boss doesn't need you anymore." Without batting an eye, the man put his gun to Devon’s chest and fired four bullets in rapid succession.

Devon stood, his face blanched white and eyes staring forward in confusion. He reached for his chest and blood covered his hand. “No!” He made a gurgling sound, then crumpled to the ground.

The horror of the scene was too much. Mira screamed as her vision blurred and tears rolled down her cheeks. She prepared to fight to keep her baby safe when she once more looked up to see a pair of shiny military boots. One of the commandos wrapped his arms around her to lift her; she fought with what little energy she had left.

This was far too like her first kidnapping. Over the man’s shoulder she got one last look at Devon, his face frozen in disbelief and blood covering his chest. She turned her head away and closed her eyes.

Chapter Twenty-Four

"Calm down, Rosita." Over the crackling line, a spate of rapid Spanish assaulted Jackson's ears. "You know I speak little Spanish." He gripped the receiver with more pressure than necessary. "What's happened?"

"They are gone." The woman's voice rose another octave."

"Who's gone? You're not making sense." His gut tightened, and his senses told him something was very wrong.

"*Señora* Mira and Charlene. *Señor* Williams is dead." Rosita's words were barely audible.

Jackson's heart nearly stopped. Dread formed in his very soul. Icy adrenaline shot through his veins. "Rafa! He shouted. "Code Red! Gather the troops"

He dropped the phone, went to the wall, and pressed the red button. Immediately, a siren sounded, letting the entire island know Alpha One had been compromised. When heard, everyone would converge on the homestead, ready to fight. He grabbed his gun and ran for the truck. Rafa was already there with the five new men and a few trainees with him.

"They've got Mira and Charlene," Jackson said between teeth clenched so hard they nearly cracked.

He took a deep breath to calm himself. Torn between focusing his mind and thinking of Charlene, he had to pull himself up hard. He'd been torn in two the last time he'd lost her, now, to lose her again—was unthinkable. Nervous energy radiated from the men in the back. He and Rafa would set the tone for the coming action. Rafa was cold-eyed and steady. He had nerves of steel and could always be counted on to do what had to be done. The men in the back were trained but rusty. He'd feel more comfortable if they'd had a few weeks practice working together. Forming a team took time. The personalities had to blend. They had to get rid of petty annoyances and become brothers. These men didn't have the time together to bond.

"How many?" Rafa pressed down on the accelerator, taking turns with wheels barely touching the ground.

"I'm not sure. Rosita was hysterical. She said they killed Devon and took Mira and Charlene." The reality of losing Charlie again nearly ripped him apart. It wouldn't matter anyhow. Brandon would tear him apart one piece at a time.

"Pull yourself together. Charlene's damn tough. I'm glad she's with Mira. With the baby so close—I'm worried." Rafa's stern eyes both prodded Jackson and showed his compassion.

Two more quick turns and they bounced to a stop. Both men were inside the house before the dust caught up to the jeep.

"Rosita?" Jackson called.

A "*Si, señor,*" told him she was in the kitchen.

He found her putting a tray of muffins into the oven. She always cooked when she was upset. She grabbed him, wrapping her thin arms around him. He held her for a minute. When she calmed, he moved her to sit at the breakfast table.

Rafa patted her shoulder and handed her a cup of tea. He sat beside her and held her hand. "Rosita," Jackson said, "we need your help. Everything you tell us could be useful. Don't leave anything out. What do you remember first that made you suspect trouble?"

"There was a phone call." Rosita's cup rattled against the spoon as she took a sip of the tea. It was *Señor* Williams for *Señora* Mira. When she spoke on the phone, she got upset. She told me there was an emergency with the orchids. She had to go immediately and check them. I… I told her Charlene was gone." She paused for a drink of tea. "The *señora* said she can't wait and left in one of the jeeps."

"Did she say what the emergency was?" Jackson asked.

"No, *señor*. Only that she was needed immediately and couldn't wait."

Rafa spoke up. "What happened next, Rosita?"

"She left and Charlene arrived about ten minutes later. I told her about *Señora* Mira, and she got upset and rushed out. She said she was going to the lab." Rosita paused and stared into space as if searching her mind for something she forgot.

"Go on," Jackson prompted.

"Then—*Madre de Dios*." Rosita crossed herself, "Then a giant helicopter landed in the yard. They waited until the jeep arrived and four men with big guns took *Señora* Falcon and *Señorita* Charlene. It was just like before in Honduras."

"What were they wearing? What did they look like?" Jackson asked. "Clothing, guns, and other details can help identify who took her."

"They had skin like mine, dark straggly hair, and

wore bandoleros across their chests. That is all I see. I hid in the pantry and saw no more."

Loud voices from the entry drew their attention away from Rosita.

Quentin waded through the crowd with Manuel in tow. "We found him tied up outside the lab."

Rafa stood and pushed Manuel into his seat. Going to the sink, he filled a glass with water and placed it in front of the man.

"Manuel got a good look at the chopper. Double rotors and heavy wide body. Sounds like a Twin Huey to me." Quentin said.

"Let's move to the conference room," Jackson said. We'll have everything we need to make our plans.

Everyone moved to the office area and sat around the conference table. There was the momentary bustle as each person claimed a seat. Jackson stood. "I am sorry to say that I have failed. Brandon put his trust in me to keep his wife and baby safe."

"You can't blame yourself for this," Quentin said. "No one alive would have suspected the little nerd of such duplicity."

"Thank you, Quentin, but I have to shoulder the blame. It happened on my watch. Now we must concentrate on getting them back. First, Rafa, you're not going to like this, but you're staying here to help people prepare and evacuate to the caves."

He noted the slight flinch Rafa made but saw no other outward signs that it bothered him. Doc was especially loved by Rafa. It was a hard choice, but Jackson couldn't leave the base and island inhabitants without a leader. You good?" he asked.

Rafa nodded.

"Tropical Storm Hector is supposed to upgrade to hurricane force winds by tonight and it's moving in our direction. Tarek, keep close tabs on its progress. Until we leave, help Rafa with the lockdown at Beta-1."

"Quentin, there's a chopper on the Beta-1 tarmac. Can you handle it? We'll move it out of the hurricane's path."

The entire group laughed at Jackson's joke. They'd move it by taking it for their trip.

Quentin laughed and swiveled in his chair. "If you have the keys, I can fly it."

"Next, Corbin, you and Joaquim load the Huey. Take gear for seven men. Put in enough rations for nine people and make that for two days. We'll just hit the local QuikStop if we run out."

"Where are we going, boss?" Joaquim asked.

"Good question. We won't exactly be flying blind. Wesley, you like electronics, right?

"Yeah, boss."

"Right then—you're on navigation and tracking."

"Tracking what?" Rafa asked in surprise. "I thought we were without eyes."

"Sorry, I never thought I'd have a need for it. It seems Brandon, being as paranoid as ever, had Charlene attach a tracker on a bracelet he bought Mira. If she is wearing it, we'll be able to find her.

"What's the range?" Corbin asked.

"We'll find out. It's a new prototype for the military. It's GPS mounted in a mini chip. She told me when she put it on the bracelet; it was barely noticeable. So we've got a good chance of picking her up. Wesley, the equipment is behind the desk. Get started. Corbin, give him a hand. The two men moved behind Charlene's desk where she had arranged the equipment on the new wall desk. Two chairs made it tight, but they managed. They quickly got the machine ready. "Boss, we're going to need the serial number for the device. Do you know where Charlene kept them?" Wesley asked.

"No, just try drawers in the desk. If anything is locked, check the key ring on my office door. She gives me all the duplicates." Jackson answered.

Corbin pulled out drawers until he found one that was locked. Quickly, he got the key ring off the door and opened it. Charlene had very carefully placed all the unused chips in numerical order.

"Damn those are small." Wesley said. "If they find it, they know what they're looking for."

"How do we know she was wearing the bracelet?" Corbin asked. He pulled a ledger from the back of the drawer and opened it. "Here they are."

Jackson stepped to look over Wesley's shoulder. "Brandon asked her to wear it until he gets back. What woman could resist such a sentimental gesture?"

"I don't know, boss. Some of the women I know would tell him yes and then do what the hell they wanted," Wesley said. "I guess Brandon got lucky and got one of the good ones."

"You're damn right he did. You need to find some different women. Let me know when you get a ping." Jackson moved to his office and sat in his chair. Keeping busy was helpful but couldn't block the worry which crawled in his stomach. He couldn't remember the last thing he'd said to her. God, he hoped it wasn't something berating. He couldn't stand that.

Charlie was an intelligent, vibrant woman who had taken him to the heights of happiness and the depths of despair. He loved her with everything he had. What the hell did he care about the past? He wanted a future. With Charlie and Hope.

He picked up the phone and dialed a very important number. "Hello, General Barnes. This is Jackson Favre of Brandon's Brigade. I need a little favor..."

Chapter Twenty-Five

Charlene woke to stifling heat, the smell of diesel fumes, and pain. Her first sight was of Mira. She ran her bound hands across her rounded belly. Her breathing became shallow little pants. Bless her heart, the poor thing was in labor. Charlene's gaze flew to Mira's face. The doctor was aware of her condition. Now what was she going to do?

Mira stopped panting and relaxed.

Sweat beaded and dripped down Charlene's face. Vibrations from the chopper and the sweltering heat caused her to pop up gagging. Her gaze darted everywhere, looking for a spot to throw up. One of the men threw her a grocery bag and she quickly relieved her nausea. While sitting, she took the opportunity to check on Mira.

"Could I have some water?" Charlene deliberately spoke in English. They didn't need to know she spoke Spanish. "Water, please."

When the man who handed her the bag didn't comply, she mimed drinking from a bottle. This time he understood and reached into a large cooler and gave her a bottle of water. A sharp reprimand came from the front. Obviously, the leader didn't want his prisoners coddled. Without consulting anyone, she scooted to Mira to have a look. She looked pale and sweaty. Hurriedly she tore a strip from the bottom of her shirt and dampened it with a little water. She placed Mira's head on her lap and wiped the cloth over her face. When her eyes fluttered open, she dribbled a little water into Mira's mouth. She gulped at the water and Charlene pulled it away.

"How are you feeling?"

"Miserable. I'm worried about the baby. I've been having Braxton Hicks contractions all day. Hopefully, that's all it is."

The man sitting beside grocery bag man kicked Charlene's foot and sent a glance toward the front. "Silencio."

Charlene glanced forward then nodded at the man. He was warning her about the wrath of the leader. She poured more water on the rag and wiped Mira's face, arms, and neck. She had to get her cooled down. Gently she put Mira's head back down and moved to her feet. She wanted to take off her sandals but was afraid the swelling would make it impossible to put them back on. Instead, she straightened Mira's legs and began rubbing them to help the circulation.

When Mira's breathing quickened, she placed a hand on her abdomen. It was tight. Charlene's worry skyrocketed. She didn't want to draw more attention to Mira than she already had. Taking the bottle of water back, she swallowed the remaining few sips. When no one said anything, she continued to sit. She had to think.

It wasn't as if Jackson and Rafa could just jump in the plane and chase them through the skies. They would have to gather supplies, and there would be little chance they could be up in the air and after them any time soon. Besides, it would take them awhile to figure out where they were headed. She'd attached the new tracking chip to Mira's bracelet, and so far, the men who'd taken them had let her keep it. Their biggest worry was the baby. Charlene was almost sure Mira was in early labor.

The helicopter slowed, made a circle, and hovered. Below them lights shined upward, and the helicopter landed. Charlene was surprised the trip had been so short. It could only mean one thing. They had landed in Honduras. There was chatter on the radio, and the headman answered. "We have a woman who needs a doctor. No—we have made our own arrangements."

Charlene heard and understood every word the man said. So, Mira was the victim and the ruse for these men to land. If one of them screamed, the radio man would assume it was the woman in pain. Not that anyone here would go out of their way to help someone. Honduras was known for its widespread corruption. Paying off the officials at the airport had been done prior to the landing. Poverty was the main ploy for such illegal acts. But not an excuse. Those who had money also had the power. The planning and execution of their kidnapping was done by someone with lots of power and money. Were they being held for ransom for some deed done by Brandon's SEAL group? He'd said they had enemies. Somehow, this seemed more personal than revenge or payback.

The doors slid open, bringing in the humid air and a spate of bugs. It was nearly dark, drawing exotic and extremely large insects. Mira squealed as one landed on her chest. Charlene brushed it off and patted Mira's hand. Two men, holding a stretcher between them, moved into the copter. They picked Mira up and set her on the stretcher. Charlene watched as they secured straps around her then carried the woman and stretcher out the helicopter.

Paper-bag man shoved her forward to follow Mira. With clumsy legs, tired from being cramped on the floor, Charlene stumbled. Immediately she was kicked from behind. The boot found her lower back. Holding back a cry of pain, she jumped up and followed more quickly.

A large, old, military truck with a covered back appeared before them. Lowering the tailgate, they slid the stretcher in. Charlene climbed in and sat beside Mira who now stopped panting and rested.

****

After refueling at Beta-1, Quentin turned the switches on the overhead display and the rotors began to whine. A quick head count then Jackson sat in the back, feeling as useless as teats on a bull. It had always been his job to fly the plane on their missions. Unfortunately, he had little training on helicopters. Quentin was a great addition to the crew. Wesley was in the copilot's seat and in charge of navigation. They had determined that Honduras was the destination of the men who'd taken the women. Right now, the kidnappers were stopped. Probably landed at the Villeda Morales Airport, which serviced San Pedro Sula. The area was urban, which wasn't a good option for recovery.

"They're on the move again," Wesley said with a very New York accent. "They're moving slow—most likely a truck or a van."

"Quentin, let's follow them all the way in the copter. We don't have time to find ground transportation, and it will give us a quicker getaway. Fly in circles if their speed is a problem."

"Gotcha, boss," Quentin answered and adjusted his speed.

Corbin sat in a drop-down cargo seat with his eyes

glued to his laptop. "Do we have any idea who took them?

Jackson ran a hand through his hair. "No, that's the damn problem. There are the usual bad guys who hate SEALs and hold a grudge, but that doesn't feel right. Since it was Mira kidnapped, I'm leaning toward the same group that took her last year. The Russians run ops through the islands and Central America all the time. The description of the perps sounds like Honduran rebels."

"What's changed? Anything new happen?" Corbin asked. "It's kind of odd for them to just show up."

Jackson raised a brow.

"The assistant," Terek replied.

"I think we can vouch for you guys and Charlene. The connection had to be through Devon. Dammit, they could have at least let him live long enough to tell us something." Jackson said.

"You're missing the point," Joaquim said. "These people wanted him dead so he *couldn't* speak."

Jackson considered Joaquim's thought. He liked to listen to all ideas and then base his decision on the information or data gathered. Except where Charlene was concerned. Adding her to the equation made it difficult to separate his feelings from his decision. "Either way, it's a gamble. We won't know how many we're up against before we go in. We know four, plus the pilot and maybe another—so at least six.

"What about the people who planned it? A lot of work went into finding and grooming Devon. Not everyone can outsmart SEALs and ex-military. Not to mention the thirty men we're training," Wesley added.

"I doubt the people behind it are in Honduras," Jackson said. "They're probably in a more congenial location. Let's concentrate on the ones who have them."

Quentin sent a worried glance behind him. "What about landing the copter? We have no idea of the terrain. It could be a city for all we know.

"Ah, there's where you're wrong. Wesley, put in the stick I gave you."

Wesley inserted the thumb drive and waited for the program to load. When the first image popped up, he whistled. "Damn, how did you get access to this?" The satellite image showed a wide-angle view of Central America. When he touched the screen, the image zoomed in to a close-up of Honduras.

Jackson smiled a wicked smile. "I called in a favor. We only have satellite access for the next four hours. That should be plenty of time to get in, neutralize the bad guys and get our ladies.

"We have a problem." Wesley turned the screen so that Jackson could see it.

"Shit! What are the coordinates and speed?" Jackson studied the image of an enormous hurricane out over the ocean, heading straight for the coast of Belize. He'd known about the storm but hadn't expected it to develop so quickly.

Wesley switched to NOA and enlarged the image. "It says it hits late tonight. Tropical storm warnings for Honduras and Mexico. Speed is ten miles per hour moving west-northwest. Winds at one-hundred-thirty miles per hour. Coordinates are latitude north nineteen degrees, twenty-one minutes, and longitude ninety-one degrees, twelve minutes west.

Only the buzz of the engine and rotors could be heard. Grim silence settled like a pall over the group. Things didn't look good. Depending upon how long it took to get the women, they might not be able to fly the return trip. Jackson allowed the enormity of the situation to sink in, then spoke. "We've all been in tight situations before. This is no different. Finding and rescuing Mira and Charlene are priority. We'll worry about the return trip when it's pertinent. We'll try to land about two clicks away from the extraction point. Any closer, and people will notice."

"At least they shouldn't hear us. The copter has been modified with some technology from area fifty-one," Quentin said.

The entire group burst into laughter. "Yeah—we've got the little green men in the trunk," Corbin spoke over the group noise.

Jackson listened as each one of the group threw out the alien quip. He was glad they were laughing instead of pensive. There'd be plenty of time for seriousness. When the laughter subsided, he spoke to Wesley. "What's the progress?"

"They're about forty-five miles northeast of Progreso in the Yoro state. If I had to guess, I'd say they're heading south to hide the women someplace rural.

"All right. We have no idea how long this will be. Get some sleep." Jackson moved up to the spot between the front seats. He'd let the men rest while he kept abreast of the situation.

Chapter Twenty-Six

Charlene sucked in a deep breath of air after the dark hood was removed. Her captor wasn't very gentle, and she lost a patch of hair. Mira, her first concern, lay on the stretcher with her eyes closed. Charlene quickly sank to her knees beside the stretcher on the floor. She touched Mira's forehead and jumped as her friend's eyes popped open.

"Are they gone?" Mira asked, her voice husky.

"For the moment. I'm not sure for how long. How are you doing?

"My contractions have slowed down, but they're getting stronger with each one. I need something to drink."

Charlene hopped up from the floor and scanned the room. The place was shabby but looked clean. Finding nothing to drink, she came back to Mira and sat beside her. "I need you to listen carefully. There's nothing to drink except water from the faucet. We can't risk that, so I'm going to have to get the attention of the men outside. There are two of them, and they have guns. I don't know what their orders are, but I think they want us alive."

Mira tried to sit up but couldn't. "They'd have killed us at the house if they wanted us dead."

"Don't." Charlene gave Mira's shoulder a gentle press. "I want them to believe you're helpless. If they don't consider you a threat, they'll leave you alone. I can deal with them, but not if I'm worried about you."

"I feel rather helpless. What do you plan to do?"

"First, I'll try to try get some water. Don't let on that you speak Spanish. That will give us a little advantage. Second, I'm going to see if there's a way out.

Mira sat up successfully and looked Charlene in the eyes. "You'll have to leave me. I can't walk far enough to get to safety. Besides, where will we go?"

"Hopefully, far enough to hide until the guys get here. There's no way I'm leaving you behind."

Mira grabbed her stomach and started panting. Charlene touched her taut abdomen and began to worry in earnest." Do you want to get up on the bed? It will be better than the floor."

"I need to walk around. It helps with the labor and quickens the contractions."

"Do we want to do that?" Charlene swallowed the hard knot which formed in her throat. She had to wrap her brain around the idea that she was going to deliver Mira's baby in just a few hours.

"We do. The sooner I have the baby, the sooner I'll be able to walk out of here."

Charlene stood and helped Mira to her feet, and she began to walk the perimeter of the room. Eight feet by ten feet. As a bedroom, it was smallish but adequate. As a prison, it was claustrophobic.

Charlene began a study of the room. The window would be best for escape. She opened the blinds to darkness. The moon provided enough light to see the wooded area behind the house. She hoped to see other houses so she could scream out the window and attract attention. Unfortunately, in Honduras that wasn't necessarily a good thing. A neighbor might be as apt to sell her on the slave market as these men were. She tried raising the window, to no avail. She rubbed her fingers along the edges and bottom of the window. It had been painted shut. If she had a knife, she could break the paint seal and open the window.

A look back at Mira brought her to the woman's side. "I forgot your water. Lie back on the bed and close your eyes. I'll get the guard's attention."

Mira grabbed her wrist and held on. "Do you really think the guys will get here in time? I'm afraid—not for me, but the baby."

"It's okay to be scared. I am. You and I are going to deliver that baby and keep it safe from our abductors." Charlene wiped a tear from Mira's face. "I promise. Now lie down and close your eyes."

Mira did as asked, and Charlene went to the door. The television blared, leaving her to guess where the two guards were. She called out. "Please, we need some water."

When no answer came, she banged her fist on the door. When that didn't elicit a response, she kicked it. The door jerked open. The man held his gun pointed Charlene. "*Silencio*."

"We need some water."

The guard shoved her back and closed the door. Charlene ignored the pain in her chest from the shove and pounded the door again. This time she made a mime of a pregnant woman and held her hand up like she was drinking.

The guard answered, "*Si*," and closed the door.

Charlene waited and waited. Finally, the door swung open and the guard, a different one this time, thrust a grocery sack into her hands. When the door slammed shut, Charlene opened the bag and perused its contents. Two large bottles of water, some sort of cola, and a large bag of chips.

"Well, we won't starve. How do you like sour cream and onion chips?"

"They are my favorite, but I don't think I should eat just now."

Charlene handed her a bottle of water and took the other. After taking a few sips, she set it aside. They might need it later. "How are your contractions?"

"Steady. You might want to time them for me." Mira stood and headed for the restroom. "I think this baby enjoys dancing on my bladder."

Charlene giggled at the way Mira sounded. "When was your last one?"

"About five minutes ago. We need to prepare."

"I'll have to ask the guards for help. I didn't like the way the tall one looked at us." Charlene said.

Mira headed to the restroom while Charlene moved to the door. Before she could knock, Mira cried out. Charlene jerked the door open and found Mira standing in front of the toilet in a puddle of water.

"Damn, damn, damn!" Mira yelled. "My water just broke."

Charlene took Mira's hand and led her out of the room. Grabbing a towel, she helped her clean up and remove her panties. She helped her to the bed where she sat on the bedside.

"I'm sorry this is happening to you right now. I've got to get some help. Lie back and rest. You're going to need your strength soon."

Charlene banged her fist against the wall and pounded her feet on the floor. She had to get the guards attention so she could help Mira.

Mira's scream filled the room, causing the guard to rush in. He pointed at Mira and covered his ears. "*Silencio*."

Charlene stuck her foot in the door to prevent him closing it. "Please we need your help. The baby is coming."

The door slammed shut, catching her foot. Rough hands pushed her foot through the opening. Pain sliced through her foot, stunning her temporarily. Slowly she got to her feet and limped over to the bed. "That was a great idea to scream. I don't think it will work twice though."

"That wasn't a pretend scream. I'm having strong labor pains."

Charlene picked up the bottle of water beside the bed and handed it to Mira. "Drink, you're getting dehydrated.

After a small sip, Mira handed the bottle back. "I think we might need this."

"Are we going to use the bed or the stretcher for the birth?" Charlene asked.

"Both. We'll lean the stretcher against the bed, creating an incline. That will make the delivery easier."

"That's smart. Why didn't I learn that in birthing school?"

"I learned it in Doctors Without Borders, though we didn't have anything as glamorous as the stretcher. When the guard comes in the next time. Let me speak to him in Spanish. I don't think we have any advantages."

Charlene wiped Mira's brow with the edge of the thin blanket. "Tell me what I need and what to do. I had an epidural; you're going to do this naturally. I know that sounds great, but it will hurt like hell. While we're waiting for the baby to come, I'm going to ask you to yell loudly so I can work on the window.

"I can do that. What are you going to use?"

I'll take a piece off the metal springs. All I need is a pointed edge to break the seal. That way, when the guys get here, they can make an easy entry."

"But what about the guns? The guys are always armed to the teeth. What about the baby?"

"Don't worry. Jackson won't let them shoot unless necessary. I need to check you."

Mira moved into position, and Charlene gently checked beneath the towel. "Dammit, Mira, you've been holding back on me. You're already fully dilated. You can scream now."

Mira let loose a bloodcurdling scream.

The door burst open, flung violently against the wall. A dangerous-looking man came in. It was neither of the prior two men. Charlene took a deep breath. They'd need to be very careful with this one.

"What is the meaning of all these screams? No one has harmed you—yet."

By the look on Mira's face, Charlene could tell she understood the danger. "*El bebé viene*," Mira explained.

The man gave a big smile and said, "Good. A blonde-haired woman is worth much more on the market if she is not pregnant."

Mira's lip quivered and Charlene cleared her throat. "Please, we need some things for the birth. Towels, a bowl of sterile water, a string, and a knife to cut the cord."

The man grinned again. "You really expect me to give you a knife?"

I must cut it. It's not like either of us can tackle the three of you. Mira is in no shape, and *I* must take care of her."

After giving Charlene a hard stare, he removed a pocketknife. Next, he pulled a lighter from another pocket. He opened the knife and used the flame from the lighter to sterilize it.

Charlene took it, making sure her fingers did not touch his.

He turned and left the room, leaving an air of menace behind him.

Charlene immediately went to Mira to offer comfort. She too realized that the men never meant for her to keep the baby.

"They're going to kill the baby," Mira said.

"Not on my watch. Right now, we need to concentrate on getting your baby into the world. We'll worry about everything else later. I need to recheck you while we still have some privacy. They will be back soon with the items I asked for. What do you think about the string? There's no way of telling where it's been."

"We'll have to sterilize it somehow. We need boiled water. I'll never take my access to betadine for granted again." Mira got up again and began walking around the room.

Charlene stripped the bed and separated the sheets from the thin blanket. The outer door slammed, and Charlene moved between Mira and the door. The door jerked opened. and the first guard came into the room. He handed Charlene a gallon of distilled water and a grocery bag with the needed items inside. There was a new roll of twine, a bottle of alcohol, a plastic bowl, two new towels, and a pack of newborn diapers. The diapers must have cost dearly in this part of the world. "Good, we got the items we need plus a little *lagniappe*. "

"That's Cajun, right?" Mira asked.

"It's Cajun for something extra. The guard put in alcohol and a pack of diapers."

"Here I was hoping for a delivery room and staff," Mira said.

"Well, milady. You're the doctor and I'm the staff. Is it about time for this little show to begin?"

Mira started panting and rubbed her belly as the contraction tightened her abdomen.

Charlene grabbed the stretcher and placed it at an angle against the bed. "Should I put one of the sheets on the stretcher?"

Mira sat on the edge of the bed. "Use the fitted sheet to go over the stretcher. No telling how much old blood is on it. Fold the pillow and put it back in the pillowcase."

Charlene did as Mira instructed and then put a piece of the string in the bowl, covering it with half the alcohol. She'd save the last for her hands. "Should we use the sheet for the baby?

Mira thought for a moment and said, "Tear the sheet in half. We'll use half to cover me and the rest to wrap the baby in."

Charlene began to pace. Not only did she fear the men in the next room, she was also nervous about delivering the baby. She'd delivered one of her own, but this was very different. Brandon would kill her if something happened to his baby on her watch. Of course, that was after he'd eliminated the rest of the squad, got into a plane, and killed all those involved with Mira's kidnapping. What were the odds of one woman being kidnapped twice? She didn't have all the data on the first kidnapping, but she'd guess they had to be related. What were they after?

"Charlene, I think it's time." Mira said gently. She patted her tummy and smiled. "I'm going to meet my little angel."

"Just never tell her how she was born." Charlene let out a nervous laugh and picked up the blanket and pillow. She placed them in the center of the stretcher so Mira could sit higher than the stretcher. It would help. She helped Mira lie down and covered her with the half sheet. Moments later Charlene checked the baby's progress. "I can see the head!" Excitement filled her. She was helping to bring a life into the world.

"I have to push," Miranda said in a panicked voice.

"You're doing great. Push!" Charlene hoped she was doing this right, but women had been doing it for millennia and survived.

Mira pushed and screamed at the same time. In between pushing she panted.

Charlene swallowed hard when the baby's head exited the birth canal. This was real.

"Push!" Charlene said above the sounds of Mira's labor. "One more time."

Mira pushed, and the baby slid out of her body into Charlene's hands.

"Is it okay?" Mira's question was nearly drowned out by the wail of the newborn baby.

"Your daughter is fine."

Charlene took care of the cord and handed the baby to Mira, then backed away, allowing mother and daughter to bond. She remembered her first moments with Hope. Her only regret now was that Jackson had not been there. No matter what wrong choices she had made, that was the one that bothered her most.

“Charlene, come meet Maxine, your goddaughter, if you say yes.”

“Yes. Now let’s get you and the baby cleaned up.”

Chapter Twenty-Seven

Jackson leaned forward and checked the screen. "Wesley is the signal strong and staying still?"

"Same as the last time, boss. It's a strong signal," he answered.

"What are we looking at for terrain?" Jackson ran a hand through his hair.

"It looks like it backs up on the jungle or a nature preserve. It's not too far from the closest town. About five miles."

"Good. Quentin? Can you plant this copter in the jungle?"

"That's my specialty, along with the desert. You give me a spot and I'll land it." Quentin turned back to the windshield.

As a pilot, especially in the military, you didn't normally get nice x's painted on a tarmac. Jackson had read Quentin's file and trusted him to land them safely. He turned to rouse the others but found them all awake checking their weapons. "All right, men. Quentin and Wesley will stay with our ride home. Corbin, Tarek, Joaquim, you're with me. I've got point, and Tarek, you've got the rear. There's to be no bullets unless necessary. I don't want someone hitting a hostage." He cringed at the word hostage, but it was best to think of her as such. He needed to keep his personal feelings out of the mission.

“We’re coming up on the coordinates now.” Wesley informed him.

Everyone had their gun in hand and were ready to deploy.

The small clearing was rough, and the landing rocked them. While Quentin and Wesley buttoned down the copter, the men filed out and formed a semicircle, guns pointing outward. Jackson checked his bearings, making sure they were headed in the right direction. Everyone put on their headsets and nodded when Jackson tested the mike. He waved a hand in a silent order and took point. The two clicks was an easy walk, even with the jungle growth.

The mountain trek ended in the backyard of a simple house. Fifty yards from the house, the men spread out and took cover. They had only a short time to wait for darkness. “Corbin, get me a heat scan.” Jackson watched the screen and saw five heat signatures. Two in the front of the house and three in the back. The third signature was a baby. Either they had the wrong house, or Mira had given birth. The notion rocked him. He would need to rethink some things and adjust the plan.

“Boss.” Corbin’s voice came over the headset. “We’ve got activity in front of the house. A single male with a drone.”

“Is this one from inside or a new one?”

“This makes three. By the way he moves, he has had training.” Corbin said.

Disappear.” Jackson whispered in the mike. The one word had the men becoming part of the scenery. Their camouflage was good enough that they wouldn’t be seen in the shadows of the greenery. Moments later, the drone turned on and buzzing filled the air. Whoever controlled the thing was doing a grid search. If it were lighter, they would be in danger of being seen. Jackson hated the wait. The time allowed for too many mistakes to happen. He'd rather just burst into the house and take back Charlene and Mira. He stopped himself from thinking those kinds of thoughts. They could get people killed. As much heartache as Charlene had brought him, he still wanted her around for a lifetime.

The last rays of the sun drifted into darkness, and still they waited. Finally, the third man entered the front room of the house. Jackson motioned Joaquim to the left and Corbin to the right. Tarek headed to the front, leaving himself to cover the rear.

Jackson waited until his men killed the kidnappers, then he moved to the back window, listened, and heard the two women's voices. The wail of a baby nearly made him slip from his precarious position. His nervousness ratcheted up another notch. Mira wouldn't be able to walk, and the baby would have to be handled carefully. He scratched on the window and waited.

"Jackson, is that you?" Charlene whispered at the tiny crack at the bottom of the window.

Somehow, she'd managed to get the window open. Reaching up, he raised the window. Charlene grabbed his head and planted a kiss on his lips. He whispered. "We've got to get out of here fast. How's Mira?"

"She'll have to be carried," Charlene said. "The baby can stay on the stretcher with her."

He'd finally reached the question he desperately needed an answer to. Had Charlene been hurt? "How are you? Those bastards didn't touch you, did they?"

"No one's touched either of us. But I'm glad we don't have to stick around," Charlene whispered.

"I need you to move, honey. Joaquim will climb inside and help lift one end of the stretcher. We'll pass her out the window to Corbin and Tarek. We'll switch back and forth during the hike. Can you keep up?"

"Yes." The one word was clipped.

Jackson turned to look at her. She was ready to meet the needs of the group, but she was scared.

"Baby, you're going to be all right. These guys can do this before breakfast."

"Jackson?" Mira called him over as the men were wrapping the blanket around her and the baby.

"Why, cher, you look radiant. Who's this little thing?" He wrapped an arm around Mira's shoulders and gave her a hug. "We've got to go, now. We'll talk on the copter."

"Wait. Charlene was knocked unconscious and had her foot hurt in the door. She might need help."

"I'm fine, Jackson. I can do this," Charlene said.

Jackson looked Charlene in the eyes. He knew she'd been trained but that was three years ago.

Charlene stood taller, her shoulders back. "I've got this, boss."

Jackson nodded, and he and Joaquim picked up the stretcher and passed Mira through the window to the other two men. Charlene crawled out, and within minutes the group disappeared into the jungle.

A warm wind began to blow by the time they reached the copter. The storm must be very large if they were feeling the tropical winds and rain. Jackson began to worry.

Wesley slid the door open on the chopper and the women were ushered quickly in out of the rain. "Get her fired up," Jackson yelled as he moved to Mira's side where she lay on the floor. The engine roared to life, and the helicopter left the ground.

"Boss this is going to be rough. The winds are right on the margin for grounding aircraft," Quentin said in a matter-of-fact voice.

"What's the latest on the storm?"

Wesley adjusted his headset and made eye contact with the men behind him. The last report looks bad. It's a strong category-two and will continue to strengthen over the next six hours to a three or higher. It's expected to hit Belize and the outer islands in less than ten hours."

"I could fly high and try to miss some of it, or we could take a jog to the west and try to outrun it," Quentin said.

The wind was too strong to be flying, but they had to make it to the island before setting down. There was no other safe place to land unless they stayed in Honduras. They had just made that impossible with the extraction of the two women. Jackson moved into the copilot's seat, ready to assist Quentin if needed. He flipped off the alarms telling them what they already knew. There was no way in hell they should be up in a copter right now. Buffeted by the high winds, the Huey struggled through the storm in a race against time.

Two and a half hours later, Jackson noticed the gas gauge. It was precariously close to empty. "Didn't you fill up before we took off?"

"I did, boss. Fighting this wind is burning up time and fuel." Quentin sounded touchy.

Jackson heard the stress in Quentin's voice. He'd had a nerve-wracking job this evening. He was starting to feel unsure. "Let's err on the side of safety. Go west and we'll outrun this storm."

****

An hour later, Jackson turned on the ground-terrain program that he'd gotten from the general. "We'll have to land closer to the caves. We can't take Mira out in the elements for long. There's a flat area below the biggest cave. Brandon had us put steps up to the cave for such an occasion as this."

"I hope he had a twin-engine chopper in mind. With the crosswinds, it's going to be dicey."

Jackson shifted in his seat so that all the men could hear him. "Gentlemen, our next move is going to be dangerous. Anyone wanting to get out now should speak up."

The men erupted in laughter.

"Well, good, then. We'll play the cards we've been dealt." As they got closer, Jackson tried the ham radio that was set up in the caves. "This is Alpha Two calling. We're near landing and are flying on fumes. Any way, we can get some lights?"

A gruff voice answered. "This is Alpha One. "We'll get down there with some flashlights."

Surprised, Jackson spoke. "Cap, when did you get home?"

"Jackson, stop talking and land that copter. Remember, my wife is onboard."

"Couldn't forget that." Jackson said.

Through the rain, a circle of lights appeared on the ground. Quentin eased the Huey into the space and cut the engines. "I need help tying the rotors down."

Jackson picked up one end of the stretcher as the door slammed open. Brandon grabbed the other end of the stretcher, and together they carried Mira and the baby out of the rain.

The cave was large and well-lit with work lights on stands. They took the stretcher to the back where medical supplies were neatly stacked.

"Oh, Brandon, I'm so glad you're home safe." Mira cried happy crocodile tears. She rolled to her side and allowed the baby's head to stick out of the sheet.

"My God," he gasped. "She or he is beautiful."

"Meet your daughter, Maxine Charlene Falcon. We're going to have a devil of a time getting her a birth certificate."

"You know how good I am with details. I love you so much, Mira."

****

Jackson looked around for Charlene and couldn't find her. His heart raced. Had she left and gone out into the storm? No one seemed to have seen her. He looked behind the medical supplies and found her. She was rolled up in a ball with a blanket covering her. She was crying. His heart nearly broke at the sound. He bent down and gently touched her shoulder.

She reacted as if she'd been slapped. "Take it easy, *cher*. It's just me. Why are you crying, Charlie?" At first, he thought she wouldn't answer, but slowly her crying slowed to a few hiccups and snuffles.

"There are too many things to name. I'm alive, saved by you and your team. I'm thankful for that. I helped bring a baby into the world. Now, I miss my own child."

The wind blew at least one-hundred-fifty-miles per hour. It was hot and wet. Everyone moved toward the back of the cave. "Why don't you get up off the floor? It'll be a muddy mess before this is over."

Charlene gave Jackson her hand. He pulled her up

and into his arms. He stared into her eyes, then lowered his head. His lips took hers in a kiss of thankfulness. She was alive and unhurt.

"Charlie, I have something to say to you." He placed his palms against her cheeks, staring into all-too-familiar eyes. "I love you with all my heart, and I want a life with you and Hope. Will you marry me?"

Charlene burst into tears again." But I messed up. I shouldn't have kept Hope from you. I should have trusted you with the whole thing."

"*Cher*, it's easy to look back and say that now. When you're living through it and your emotions are in turmoil, you make decisions that you normally would not. I don't care about the past. I want you now. In the present."

Charlene feathered kisses along his jaw. "I can't wait for you to meet Hope."

"Well?" Jackson gave her a serious look and waited.

"Yes, Jackson. I'll marry you and make a family with you and Hope."

Hours later, the jeep made slow progress over the debris field left by the storm surge. Charlene surveyed the damage from the front seat while Brandon and Mira cuddled with their baby in the back. Jackson stopped the jeep and jumped out to remove a large limb blocking the road. Before he could touch the limb, a chorus from one of the training songs broke the silence. Quentin and the other men grabbed the limb, threw it onto the side of the road, then moved forward. They cleared the trail as the jeep slowly followed them.

The air had a surreal quality to it. Monkeys and other climbers created quite a racket as the jeep passed. After an hour of tense driving, they reached the old plantation house. A large palm tree had landed on the roof above the living room and front veranda. Jackson and Brandon jumped from the jeep and headed for the house. Charlene gave Mira a questioning look, and at her nod she left to follow the men.

"It's not too bad on the outside. A few new rafters and new roofing and she'll be fine," Brandon said.

"Doesn't look too bad. Let's look inside." Jackson said.

Charlene eyed the tree and thought both men were being optimistic. Thankfully, as they walked through the door there were few signs of storm surge. There was a large puddle below where the tree had broken through the ceiling, and that was the extent of the damage.

Brandon made a beeline for the door and his wife and daughter.

Jackson took Charlene by the arm. "Why don't you and Miguel go check out the lab. The code is 1109. I know it's simple, but at the time we were trying to get things going. Here are the duplicate keys. I'll check out the offices and see how they fared."

Charlene turned to go, but Jackson still held her arm. She turned back, and he pulled her up against his chest. "I can't wait until tonight." He softly kissed her lips and let her go.

Chapter Twenty-Eight

Charlene shook her head to clear his potency from her mind. She spotted Miguel on the porch. "Let's go check out the lab."

The jeep ride took longer than normal. Quentin and the men were still working to remove the limbs and other objects from the track. Soon, they drove up next to the door of the lab. She walked with Miguel around the back to check the nursery. Here, there was damage. The tables had been blown over and many were shredded by the wind.

"Thank God you put the plants inside. They'd have never made it out here."

"*Si, senorita.* I had to save the *señora's* plants. She is important, and one day she will find a cure for some disease."

"You're right. Why don't you work out here so we can bring the plants back out. I'll go check the lab. Her heart pounded as she reached the door and placed her fingers on the knob. "Devon is dead," she murmured like a mantra. She was nervous about going through the door.

The doorknob turned easily, bringing a moment of trepidation—then she remembered. Devon wouldn't have cared if the door locked behind him. After entering the code for the second door, she opened it cautiously. She didn't remember pulling her gun, but there it was in her hand and in the proper siting position.

Charlene holstered her gun and stepped warily around the rows of plants lining the floor. Even in a hurry Miguel had followed scientific protocol. Once more, she used the code to open Mira's office. Besides the overturned desk chair, things were like they always were when she came to the lab. Miguel had brought the box that contained Mira's original Blue Spider Orchid that Devon had taken. It sat atop the lab table. All was right with Mira's world.

Charlene went back to check on Miguel. He had the entire area picked up. "Will the plants be okay until tomorrow?" she asked.

"*Si*, we can wait until then. I'll go help the other men pick up limbs."

As she turned the curve in the track, she heard a large helicopter fly over and land at the camp. That would be the trainees coming back. Things were getting back to normal. She drove on and parked in front of the house. Mira and Brandon were each in a rocker on the porch. She felt a pang in her womb. She wanted her baby. "You two look like a picture for a family-home magazine."

"Only if the photo is of two tired old parents," Mira said. "What about the lab? Is everything okay?"

"If you don't calm down, I'm going to tell Charlene to forget about her report," Brandon teased.

"The lab is fine, Mira. I had Miguel leave the seedlings inside until you decide what to do. Did the team figure out why we were kidnapped?"

Brandon looked uncomfortable. "That would be my fault. When I extracted Max, Mira's uncle, the Russians retaliated by taking you and Mira. They figured I'd give up Max if they threatened my wife."

Charlene shook her head. "Hopefully, no one else is mad at you."

"I'm afraid it goes with the job."

"Brandon," Charlene asked. "How do I get my daughter here quickly? Jackson and I are to be married. We both want her here for the ceremony."

"A wedding! I knew you two were meant for each other." Mira handed the baby to Brandon. "When is it?"

"Whenever we can get Hope here and arrange everything." Charlene looked to the door where Jackson was making his way out."

"You've got that right. The two of us have lost enough time. I can't wait to meet my daughter." Jackson pulled Charlene up against his chest, resting his chin upon her head.

Brandon put the baby on his shoulder and patted her back. "Give me the details, and I'll take care of it right now. Mira's uncle Max is coming also. He was my mission. We'll have one big celebration."

Charlene sniffled. Everyone was being so nice.

Jackson turned her around and kissed her wet cheeks. "There's no need to cry, *bebe*. Everything's going to be all right."

Charlene swiped her cheeks. "I know. It's just that I'm so happy."

"Let's go give your aunt a call. Then Brandon can make arrangements. He's good at that."

****

Jackson wiped the sweat from his palms as he eased the plane onto the water. He taxied to an empty dock slip and turned the plane off."

"I can't believe how nervous you are," Charlene laughed.

"Don't forget excited. It's not every day a man gets to meet his daughter for the first time. Do you think she'll like me?" Jackson grabbed the teddy bear and spray of flowers from the seat in the back.

"She's going to love you. Why can't you believe me?"

Jackson locked the plane and helped Charlene onto the dock. "What did you tell her about me, *cher*?"

Charlene looked uncomfortable for a moment before speaking. "I told her that you were serving your country and would come home when you were through."

"Did she accept that?"

"There are times when she accepts that her daddy can't be at home with us. Other days she's sad. I knew one day that I'd have to explain better, but she's so young."

Jackson bundled the flowers and bear against his chest and took Charlene's hand in his. "I don't want you to beat yourself up over this. We're officially starting over, remember?" They entered the airport terminal and made their way to the appropriate gate.

Charlene squeezed his hand and took a seat. "I'm a work in progress. It may take some time to face all the things that have happened and how I reacted."

Jackson checked the arrival schedule on the overhead screen then glanced at his watch. Five minutes. It seemed a lifetime before the screen flashed that the flight had arrived. Jackson jumped to his feet and crushed the flowers and bear against his chest. Charlene took his hand in hers and gave it a squeeze. Jackson squeezed back and planted a quick kiss on her cheek. He scanned the group of people streaming through the arrival door and stiffened when a smallish woman holding a child's hand moved into view.

When Charlene dropped to her knees, the beautiful child ran into her mother's arms. Tears streamed down Charlie's face and Jackson realized his own cheeks were damp.

Jackson handed the woman the spray of slightly squished flowers. "Welcome to Belize, Mrs. Bowman. Charlie has told me so much about you. Thanks for taking care of Hope and Charlie during their trying time. I plan to spend the rest of my life making things up to them."

"Well, Jackson, I'm happy to be here, and I'm so glad things have worked out for you two. My niece and Hope deserve the best. I plan on checking on them often."

"We'll be happy to have you any time."

Charlene stood and led Hope to Jackson. "Remember I said I had a surprise for you? Well, this handsome man is your surprise. This is your daddy, Hope."

As surprise followed by happiness flashed over Hope's face, Jackson bent down and handed the teddy bear to the little girl—his daughter. His heart squeezed with emotion. This little angel was part of him. He stood, and Hope moved to him and wrapped her arms around his legs.

"I can't believe I have a daddy like all the other kids."

Jackson swooped down and picked the child up. She wasn't afraid of him. Hope looked him in the eye and placed her little hands on each of his cheeks and asked, "Are you really my daddy? Mommy said you were handsome and strong."

"Yes, *cher*, I'm your daddy. I'm so glad to finally meet you. Your mommy told me you were beautiful and had my eyes. What do you think? Can we be friends?"

"Of course, Daddy, we're family."

Charlene grabbed the small suitcase and slipped her arm through her aunt's arm.

Jackson swelled with pride as he led his ladies to baggage claim.

****

Three days later, Charlene pinned the circlet of flowers and ribbons to her daughter's curls. She smoothed down the folds on her taffeta-and-chiffon dress and lastly added the puka-shell necklace Jackson had given his daughter.

Charlene slipped on her own dress. The off-shoulder style hugged her figure at the top, and the bottom flared out with a small train. The bodice was filled with intricate embroidery. She couldn't wait for Jackson to see it. After a last-minute check of her hair and her own puka-shell necklace, she made her way to the gazebo. Jackson stood at the front, waiting for her to walk to him. His eyes flared with a hungry look as he devoured the image of her in the dress. She sent a heated look back to him and smiled her brightest smile.

Aunt Jenny patted her hand and let her continue up the aisle alone. When she reached Jackson, he took her hand and led her to the altar. The priest was Belizean and performed the ceremony with efficiency and care. At the words, "Will you love each other," both she and Jackson had to wipe away tears. Hope happily spilled flower petals where she walked and finally put the basket down and stood between the two of them, holding tight to her mommy's hand.

"I pronounce you man and wife," the priest said.

"Forever, *cher*," Jackson whispered for her ears only. And then they were all hugging. The three of them. Together.

"Hey, save some of that for us. We get to kiss the bride," Rafa called out."

Jackson pulled back from her lips and lifted Hope into his arms. He kissed her cheek and handed her to Rafa. "Here's all the sugar you can handle."

Unperturbed, Rafa placed a sloppy kiss on the child's cheek and passed her to the next in line.

"Don't spoil her," Charlene waved to Hope and turned for a kiss from Brandon and Mira. Rafa, not to be outdone, pulled her in for a kiss lightly on the lips. Charlene flushed as Jackson growled.

"That might just be your last kiss, Rafa," Jackson growled again and pulled her into his arms.

Charlene followed Mira and made it to the reception which sprawled from the dining room through the living room and out to the veranda. All the trainees and new recruits had been invited. Though crowded, everyone had a great time. Mira was ecstatic with Max's arm around her shoulder.

"Ladies and gentlemen." Brandon got everyone's attention. "I'd like to propose a toast. To a man who saved my life and has been my lifelong friend. May you and your bride find happiness and peace forever. To Jackson and Charlene!"

The crowd roared and lifted their drinks.

Aunt Jenny caught the bouquet, and Jackson took Charlene's arm and led her to Mira. Together, the two went into the main-floor bedroom. She changed into shorts and a shirt. Out of habit, she put her gun at her back. She met Jackson outside, where the jeep and Rafa waited. They took off, heading for *Darlin.* Before long, they were up in the air.

"Where are we going?"

"We're going to fly into the sunset and land on our favorite caye. Nothing fancy. You all right with that?"

Charlene reached for his hand and gave it a squeeze. "I'll fly into the sunset with you any day you want. I don't need fancy. I need you and your love."

Jackson reached over and gave her a kiss. "*Laissez les bon temps rouler.*"

A word about the author…

Evelyn Timidaiski is a Golden Palm winner, Winter Rose finalist, and author of the series Brandon's Brigade. Her sense of adventure, deep-rooted values, and love of romance enliven her fast-paced novels.

Ms. Timidaiski lives with her Pomeranian, Chloe, in Mississippi, where she writes romantic suspense, contemporary, and fantasy. When she isn't painting or taking nature photographs, you will find her at her computer, crafting her newest novel.

She loves to hear from readers and can be reached at: http://www.evelyntimidaiskiauthor.com

Thank you for purchasing
this publication of The Wild Rose Press, Inc.

For questions or more information
contact us at
info@thewildrosepress.com.

The Wild Rose Press, Inc.
www.thewildrosepress.com